Gigantic Death Worm

THE NEW BIZARRO AUTHOR SERIES

PRESENTS

Gigantic Death Worm

VINCE KRAMER

Eraserhead Press
Portland, OR

ERASERHEAD PRESS
205 NE BRYANT
PORTLAND, OR 97211

WWW.ERASERHEADPRESS.COM

ISBN: 1-62105-004-1

Printed in the USA.

Editor's Note:

Brace yourselves. This is one hell of a ride down a mountain of hilarity.

If you don't know Vince Kramer, this book is a great introduction to a unique and AWESOME individual. He and I lived together when he wrote Gigantic Death Worm. He came up with the idea when we were talking about utterly stupid that movie, *Frozen*, is. Or at least I thought it was stupid. Maybe he hadn't seen it yet and I was talking him out of watching it. I don't know. But I DO know that I hate that stupid movie. I mean, really, come the fuck on. Ski hills don't get completely abandoned for a week. Wolves don't live at resorts. I've personally jumped from the lift with skis on more times than I can count.

Anyway, we talked about how dumb it was and about the lack of wolves in real life, and somehow Vince came up with the ABSOLUTELY INSANE IDEA that wolf-spitting bears would be far more badass, and much more of a threat to freezing idiots on a ski lift. The idea of wolf-spitting bears made me roll around on the floor laughing, and then Vince went OFF. This story was born from crazy laughter. I watched Vince write it—acting it out with action figures, and trapping himself away with no internet, TV, or phone for days on end. This book is written like only Vince could write it. It is seriously bad ass. It's pretty much TOTALLY FUCKING AWESOME.

I'm happy to present Vince Kramer's book to you as part of the New Bizarro Author Series. This is this author's first book! The NBAS strives to bring new voices in bizarro fiction to our readers. It serves as an opportunity to introduce you to new writers, and to introduce them into the world of being an author. Eraserhead Press is happy to bring new, weird voices to you in the hopes that these authors will prove themselves to be strong members of the bizarro community and continue to entertain you for years to come. The publishing of this book marks the beginning of a one year proving period. Please help support our NBAS writers in their endeavors by telling your friends about their cool new books. This book you hold is only one of several hundred that must be sold in order for this author to continue on his path. We hope you help him along as best as you can. Thank you.

~~Kevin Shamel

Author's Note:

I'd like to dedicate this book to my oldest friend, Carlton Mellick, for telling me I should write a book, and to Kevin Shamel, for making me actually do it. This book wouldn't have been written without their constant encouragement, expertise, and advice. And also to Cameron Pierce, and again to Carl, for letting me in on how you can write a book in just 3 days. And finally, to Jeff Burk, for thinking this crazy shit was hilarious. Thanks a million to you all, you godlike gods of Bizarro. You rule!

I'd also like to thank the following people for their friendship, love, and support. Life wouldn't be the same without you -

Zack Emery, Ray Kelley, Kevin L. Donihe, Rose O'Keefe, David Agranoff, Erik Jagos, Jason Eminhizer, Eric Hendrixson, David Chadwick, Danny Chadwick, Christian Erickson, Bradley Sands, Kirk Jones, Anthony Wakefield, Anna Searles, Larry Curl, Robert Hase, LeAnn Romans, Andrew Freudenberg, Rachel Roeske, John Burke, Rachel E. Graves, Chrissy Horchheimer, Mykle Hansen, Jason Wuchenich, Garrett Cook, Constance Ann Fitzgerald, Mike Conklin, Jordan Krall, Jason Kull, Kirsten Alene Pierce, Jess Gulbranson, Shane Bridges, Steve Lowe, Dan Minor, Heidi L. Kostura Brewer, Benjamin Burton, William Pauley III, Owen Carr, Jonas Grey, Nick Cioffi, Ruby Payne, Peter Hagerty, David Cordray, Joseph Kenneth, Sam Reeve, Michael Allen Rose, Karl Fischer, Zoë Welch, Keith Mengelkoch, Jeremy Johnson, Bruce Taylor, David W. Barbee, Ash Lomen, Kelly Godinez, Brent Millis, Matthew Revert, Cody Goodfellow, John Skipp, Terri Plewa, Jon Hanna, and Justin Huffhines.

And to my loving family – My dad, Budd Kramer, my mom, JoAnn Kramer, my sister Jody, Jay Perry, my niece Sarah, my nephews Jared and Alex, and to all my grandparents, aunts, uncles, and cousins back in Philly. Miss you guys.

Part 1

Chapter One

"So, how are the brain parasites doing?"

Dave had brain parasites. He wasn't very happy about it.

"Terrible. Sometimes I feel like they're ripping me apart inside. They're driving me crazy, and the medication isn't working. It's hopeless. I don't know what to do."

Mike tried to look at him with a serious face, then broke-up and started laughing. "*WAH WAH WAH,* I have *BRAIN PARASITES, WAH WAH WAH!* THAT'S WHAT YOU SOUND LIKE, DUDE!" He kept laughing.

Dave just hung his head in shame.

"Well bro, all you need to do is keep drinking and getting high. Keep your mind off your fucking brain, man. That's stupid. Look, Suzanne's on her knees now."

Mike motioned toward the ski-lift. The blizzard had finally stopped, which meant they could get down in time to make the party on campus. But they were broke and just needed return lift-tickets. Mike's girlfriend was on her knees giving the ski-lift operator a blowjob. Mike and Dave pulled down their pants, leaned against the ski-rack, and started masturbating in unison. A couple of kids walking by on the hill stopped and stared. Mike noticed.

"What the fuck are you looking at, you fucking brats! GET!" Mike yelled, throwing an empty beer bottle at them. It whizzed past one of their heads.

The kids yelped and scattered toward another gang of children who were watching the fat guy getting his dick sucked. They were pointing and seemed to be engaged in some sort of serious discussion about it.

Mike moaned. Dave took a quick glance at his small cock, making sure not to stare. Mike was very sensitive about it.

Fuck. Now all I'm thinking about is cock. Dave looked back to the x-rated ski-lift scene. *If only I could see her tits. Man, I wish I could cum all over those tits.*

At that second, as if on cue, Mike jizzed all over the snow, letting out an echoing howl that turned the head of every deer within range. They didn't like that and ran the fuck out of there. Mike's hot liquid semen melted the snow, creating miniature canyons. It looked interesting.

"Christ. I needed that," he said.

Sometimes Dave was really embarrassed to be around Mike but would never show it. They'd been best friends all semester no matter how much of a dick he always was. And Dave thought he was kind of cool anyway. Maybe he didn't actually give a fuck about being embarrassed about Mike.

(He didn't, he loved Mike. —*The Narrator*)

Mike was Dave's roommate and only friend in college. Mike was a huge asshole jock frat boy and was annoying as all hell, but Dave stuck to him like glue because Mike could ALWAYS get him high, ALWAYS get him drunk, and would always take him to the best parties. Dave hated college. All he wanted to do was get fucked up. Especially after what happened on vacation.

Suzanne walked back along the snowy path, wiping her mouth. In the distance, the fat, ugly, disgusting-looking ski-lift operator with a moustache was fastening his belt. Dave put his dick back in his pants when he saw her approach. He was not only cock-shy but nervous around her. He needed a drink pretty bad.

"Ew!" She spit. "His cum tasted all mungey."

"I hate when that happens," Dave said, regretting the words the second they left his mouth.

She gave him a bitchy glare, thinking he was making fun of her.

"Shut up, Dave! You fuck..." She adjusted her boobs, and then looked to her boyfriend and smiled. "I got the lift-tickets for going back down. And not only that, but a case of Bud Light, a joint, a Hershey's Bar, a lollipop and everything. Hell, I think I deserve a goddamn TROPHY for that."

She didn't mean that in the way like how terrible it was that she had to blow some big, fat, ugly guy for lift tickets, but in the way that she was actually proud of being a good cocksucker and should be rewarded. It would just feel nice to be recognized every once in a while.

"Well, fuckin' A! Let's get shitfaced and party! Dave, grab our shit." Mike kicked over their skis, boards and poles and went to join Suzanne. When she went to kiss him, he turned his cheek and said, "Gross, babe."

Dave picked up their shit and followed them over to the ski-lift. He was looking forward to relaxing and pounding some beers on the way down. But he sure as hell wasn't going to drink a Bud Light. The threesome piled into the ski-lift chair with their gear. Mike pulled down the safety bar. The ski-lift mechanism whirred into motion.

As they passed the ski-lift operator, he rubbed his nipples suggestively and said, "Have a good time going DOWN."

"HOLY SHIT!" complained Suzanne. "It's fucking COLD up on this mountain." She went, "*BRRRRR.* Give me a fucking beer!"

Mike grabbed a Bud Light out of their mini-cooler, popped the cap with his teeth, and handed it to her. Then he did the same for himself and Dave. When no one was looking, Dave dropped his bottle of Bud Light off the side of the chair. It landed straight-up in the snow. Suzanne had already slammed her entire beer by that time and let out a huge belch.

"Damn, woman!" exclaimed Mike. "First cum breath, now a beer-belch. Good thing you're pretty, babe, or I'd knock your fucking teeth in." He laughed hysterically about his joke and fumbled for another beer for her.

Dave was staring off into the black distance, oblivious to them and in his own world. He drank deeply from his Arrogant Bastard, thinking it was a good starter beer because of the high alcohol content. The chair swayed side-to-side a bit as Mike messed with the beer cooler. He produced another Bud Light for Suzanne and one for himself.

"Fucking A!" he said, putting his arm around Suzanne. "Bet we can finish off this whole case between the two of us before we reach the bottom! Forget about Dave, he's a fucking lightweight." He tweaked her nipple and sighed.

Suzanne giggled in agreement, snorting on her beer, and shot a 'You're lame' glare over to Dave.

Dave felt hurt but was already on to a bottle of Dogfish Head 90-Minute IPA. He decided to focus on that and weed. "Are we going to get high or what?" he asked.

"Fuck yeah! Break out, Suze!"

She threw an empty beer bottle at a tree, hitting it dead on. It shattered, greatly upsetting an owl. In our language, his hoot would've translated into, "What the *fuck*?!"

"Damn, I almost forgot," she said as she rummaged through her pockets.

They started passing around the joint. When it got to Dave, he crumbled it up and put it in the bowl of a three-foot-tall water bong. Everyone exclaimed how awesome that was.

At the top of the mountain, in the control booth, the ski-lift operator snorted a huge line of coke off a porn star's tits in a really awesome nudie magazine. He pulled his head up and yelled, "THAT'S THE SHIT!" and kept on masturbating, his pants well down around his ankles. He couldn't wait to close up for the night, get home, sit down, pull down his pants, look at a porno mag, beat off, smoke pot and drink beer. He didn't mind giving all of his Bud Light to the pretty blonde girl with the big fake tits because he had a whole bunch of coke to snort. His life felt awesome.

A big, black, snarling shape ran at the ski-lift operator from behind and slashed him to death before he could even hear it coming. The ugly fat guy screamed in horror as he was thrashed around the booth. Blood sprayed all over the windows. In seconds his dead body fell atop the control panel with a slamming thud and was dragged away into the darkness. A deer watching nearby almost pissed himself. It was so fucking terrifying, he decided to never come back there again and left.

The ski-lift came to a grinding halt. The threesome screamed as it rocked violently back and forth. Mike held onto the water bong for dear life. The giant spotlights on the ski-lift poles blacked out one by one. Everything went silent.

"WHAT THE FUCK?!?!" Mike screamed.

"OH MY GOD!!" yelled Suzanne. "IS THE BONG OKAY?!"

"I think so."

"Whew, that was a close one."

Dave assessed the situation. "Guys, I think we're in a little bit of trouble here."

Chapter Two

"Shut up, Dave. It's probably just a malfunction. The ski-lift will be working again in no time." Mike offered him a beer.

Dave smacked it out of his hand. "Fuck your Bud Light and FUCK YOU! You don't understand! The whole place is closed until next weekend! We're stuck up here! The temperature is dropping fast! We'll freeze to death!"

Mike went wild-eyed. "AND WE'LL STARVE! HOLY SHIT! Suzanne, where's your fucking chocolate!" He went after her, shaking her violently and trying to search her pockets.

She started kicking and screaming. "WHAT THE FUCK ARE YOU DOING, ASSHOLE?!!! IT'S *MY* CHOCOLATE BAR! You ain't getting any of it, you motherfucking piece of shit!"

Mike nestled back in his seat, defeated.

"Christ, guys. Relax. Here, have some cheeseburgers." Dave handed them some cheeseburgers, wrapped in white paper with a giant yellow "M" on them. "Now let's think of a way out of here…"

"One of us is going to have to jump, then walk down to the bottom and get help," Mike said, enjoying his delicious cheeseburger.

Dave looked over the railing. "Dude, it's like a hundred-foot drop. You'll die."

Mike psshawed him. "I jump off these things all the time,

14

dude. I'll land on my feet and just board down."

"You'll break your legs!"

Suzanne belched and threw her wadded-up paper wrapper off the lift. It landed next to an array of empty beer bottles and napkins. A squirrel chittered and did an angry dance. "He's right. I saw it in a movie once," she said.

"So what are we going to do, Mr. Smarty-Pants?" Mike asked.

Dave thought for a second. "You'll have to climb down. Now, we don't have any rope, but we can take off our clothes and tie them together, super tight-like. Then we'll have a rope."

"But we'll also be *naked*," Suzanne pointed out. "We'll still freeze to death while you're down there looking for help! Fuck, you'll probably be eaten by wolves!"

"There's no fucking wolves on this mountain, dude," Mike said. "This is Arizona."

"He's right. But there's bears."

They both looked at Dave and laughed.

"Bears!" Mike made his hands into bear claws, snarled and went *RAWR!*

Dave shielded his face.

"Yeah, right, dude. Look—there's *no* wolves, there's *no* bears, there's just three people on a mountain starving to death and dying of thirst." Mike finished the last bite of his cheeseburger and chased it down with another Bud Light. "And we'll be freezing to death if we don't go down the mountain and get more beer."

"You mean call for help," Dave reminded him.

"Yeah, but... uh, I'll bring back some more beer and shit. SHUT UP!" Mike stood up and started unfastening his belt. "Now let's get naked!"

"WHOOOO!" exclaimed Suzanne.

The threesome was nude and shivering. Suzanne was going,

"*BRRRR!*" but in a far bitchier tone. All their clothes, including scarves and socks and underwear, were tied together in crude knots.

Dave checked it over. "Yeah, seems like we have about a hundred feet here."

"Well, then what are we waiting for?" Mike grabbed the end of the rope that had Suzanne's big pink bra attached to it. "Geronimo!"

Mike jumped off the ski-lift heroically, determined to look cool.

Dave gasped.

The line of rope quickly disappeared off the lift all snake-like. It wasn't tied to anything. Dave watched in shock as his boxers at the other end of the rope slipped off the chair and into the darkness.

Then he and Suzanne heard a loud thud.

"HOLY SHIT! YOU WERE SUPPOSED TO TIE THAT DOWN YOU FUCKER!" Suzanne screamed, punching Dave in the arm.

"We didn't even get to that part yet!"

Suzanne gave him another *you're a stupid motherfucking bastard* look and peered down over the rail.

"Mike?!" she yelled. "Are you okay? MIKE?!?!"

They heard a loud whoop.

Dave shined a flashlight down. Mike was down there, standing on two feet, totally fine. Completely naked, but totally fine.

"FUCK YEAH! THAT WAS AWESOME!"

"HOW THE HELL DID YOU SURVIVE THE FALL?" Dave yelled loudly, so he could hear him. "WE HADN'T EVEN TIED THE ROPE DOWN, YET!"

"I LANDED IN THE SNOWBANK, DUDE! THE SNOW'S SOFT! IT CUSHIONED MY FALL! DURH! THAT'S HOW SNOW WORKS!"

"WHOO-HOO!" exclaimed Suzanne, all happy as shit. "MIKE! WHEN YOU GET TO THE STORE GET SOME JAEGER AND RED BULL! AND SOME POTATO CHIPS AND SHIT! AND HURRY THE FUCK UP!" Suzanne was

16

wearing a long fur-coat. She smiled. "OH, AND WATCH OUT FOR WOLVES! OOOOOH!"

Mike said, "YOU MEAN BEEAAAARRRSSS!!!!"

Suzanne and Mike started laughing their asses off.

Dave sat back in his chair, red with embarrassment. And he was uncomfortable in his three-piece Armani suit.

Mike untied his clothing from the big long rope and got dressed. Then he turned to walk down the mountain and was suddenly faced by a gigantic bear. He stopped dead in his tracks.

The bear was huge. It must've weighed two tons. But the bear didn't need to know math to have confidence in itself.

(It was a Black Bear, native to the mountainous area of Flagstaff, Arizona. There are pretty much bears everywhere up there. And they're extremely dangerous so never go outside. *–The Narrator*)

Mike was face to face with the monstrous beast. Its solid black eyes gave him the look of death. It growled an angry growl from a mouth of clenched teeth—razor-sharp teeth, that were all pointy and scary.

"MIKE. DON'T MOVE." Dave yelled cautiously, trying to think of a plan.

Mike took a few steps back, slowly pissing the bear off more and more with each step.

"DUDE! THROW ME SOMETHING TO FIGHT WITH! ONE OF THE SKI-POLES... MY BOARD... *ANYTHING!*"

The bear heard all of this loud yelling and kept advancing. It was a bear.

"OKAY!" Dave said.

A big snowboard fell from the sky and hit Mike square in the head. He yelled out in pain and fell over. He looked up at the lift and yelled, "WHAT THE FUCK, DUDE!?"

"Sorry!"

Suzanne laughed and took a bong hit. Then she picked up her cell phone and started filming the scene below.

"DAVE! MORE LIGHT," she said impatiently.

"OKAY."

Dave held the light on Mike. He was pulling himself backward on the palms of his hands as the bear slowly came toward him, snarling.

Dave dangled the ski-poles over the chair. "MIKE! WATCH OUT! I'M GOING TO DROP THE POLES!"

Dave dropped the poles. One landed a few feet away in the snow. The other landed straight up in Mike's leg, piercing it sharply. He let out an ungodly shriek of pain. The squirrel nearby pointed at him and laughed, thinking that he got what he deserved.

"DUDE! WHAT THE FUCK?!" Mike yelled again, twice as pissed off this time.

"Sorry!"

Suzanne laughed so hard she almost fell over. She continued filming.

The bear looked up and noticed them for the first time.

"MIKE! PULL THE SKI-POLE OUT OF YOUR LEG AND STAB THE BEAR IN THE THROAT WITH IT! THAT SHOULD KILL IT!"

Mike grabbed the ski-pole stuck in his leg and tried hard to yank it out. But it was too painful, and he screamed.

Suzanne laughed. "PUSSY!"

"I CAN'T DO IT, DAVE!" Mike cried. "THROW ME SOMETHING ELSE!"

"OKAY!" Dave fumbled around for something else.

The bear looked up to Dave and Suzanne, back down to Mike, and then back up to Dave and Suzanne again. They were all testing the bear's patience and he was getting sick of it. The bear decided he would probably attack soon, but he was kind-of interested in what was going on up in the ski-lift.

Then, from out of nowhere, a ridiculously large samurai sword fell on Mike's legs, cutting them off at the knees.

Mike let out a blood curdling scream. This shocked even

the bear. "MY LEGS!"

Dave gasped. "I'M SORRY!"

Suzanne's jaw dropped open. "OH MY GOD!" She got pissed off and started punching Dave in the arm. "YOU KILLED HIM YOU BASTARD!"

"No, wait! He'll be fine! He can bandage his legs after he kills the bear with the sword! Just watch!" Dave yelled down to Mike, "MIKE! KILL THE BEAR WITH THE SWORD AND THEN BANDAGE YOUR LEGS WITH SOME CLOTHES! DON'T WORRY! YOU'RE GOING TO BE TOTALLY FINE!"

Mike gasped and grabbed the samurai sword. He held it up to the bear, as if to say, "Fuck you, bear!"

The bear stood up on its legs and roared, then slapped the sword out of Mike's hands. Mike screamed. The bear came down on top of him, pinning him with its front legs. It snarled.

Dave tensed, looking down on what was about to be his friend's demise. "NOOOOOOOOO!!!!!!" he yelled.

Suzanne looked over the rail, choking on a bong hit.

Mike looked up right into her eyes. "SUZANNE! I LOVE YOU!!"

Suzanne took a chug of a Sam Adams, belched, and looked down at her boyfriend. "YOU HAVE A SMALL DICK!"

Then the bear ate his face off, and he died from it.

Chapter Three

Dave woke as the sun rose over the mountain. He'd given Suzanne a bunch of sleeping pills the night before to calm her the fuck down. She was flipping out because her mom scolded her for posting a video of Mike's death on Facebook. The tirade Suzanne flew into about how much she hated her parents drove Dave nuts.

He felt terrible. There were several sharp, digging pains in his head. He needed his medication badly. He started to get terribly worried about what might happen if he didn't get it soon. He shrugged off the thought and decided some nice breakfast might cheer him up. He broke some eggs over the grill and put on a pot of coffee.

Suzanne woke to the smell of delicious breakfast, got up, and stretched.

The ski-lift chair swayed side-to-side.

Dave held onto his tiny grill with his oven mitts.

The bear had come back several times during the night to eat little pieces of Mike. In his head, Dave could hear Mike's screams mixed with the crunching and tearing sounds of the bear chewing on his departed friend's legs, arms and torso. He had gotten very drunk and had a flashback of all the good times he shared with Mike. He set the flashbacks to the song, *Summer of '69*, by Bryan Adams.

Hope for getting off the mountain dwindled. Dave checked the internet on his cell phone for the number to the

Ski Chalet, but kept getting voice mail every time he called. It was a waste of time. He considered grappling across the wire to the next ski-lift chair, which was close to a pole that had ladder rungs running down it. But he was really hung over and it seemed like that would take a lot of effort.

Dave sighed and emptied the portable toilet over the side of the chair. A deer thought he was marking his territory and was kind of mad because that's where he always started his morning walk.

Dave and Suzanne spent the rest of the day watching a DVD of the fourth season of the show, *Friends*, and then prepared for another dark, cold, and scary night. By getting some more pot and a keg of Heineken.

The bear came back after dusk to finish what remained of Mike's frozen corpse, which wasn't much. He was happy it was just how he left it.

Dave noticed his return. "Suze! Look, he's back!"

"So what? I'm so over it." She went back to texting her friend about who was cuter—Joey or Chandler. Ross wasn't even in the mix.

Two more bears joined the scene below, converging from separate directions. The first bear stood up on its legs and roared as if to say, "Mine! Fuck off!" The other bears roared too, rising up to the challenge.

"Suzanne! Look!" Dave swatted Suzanne on the shoulder. "More fucking bears!"

"Holy shit!" she said, looking over the lift-rail, suddenly interested again.

The bears flew into a terrifying and violent death match, the kind that can only be seen and not fully described in detail. Every once in a while a challenging bear would get to the remains of Mike's corpse and make away with an arm or leg bone or internal organ. The one that swallowed the stomach made a disgusted face and puked. That was definitely the worst part of his evening thus far.

They kept fighting and fighting. It looked awesome.

While they were distracted, a giant owl swooped down and grabbed the last piece of Mike's body and flew away with it. It went, "Hoot-Hoot!" (English translation: *Ha-ha, fuck you guys!)*

The bears looked up, dumbfounded. And angry. Very, VERY angry. *What now?* thought the bears.

The first bear noticed the couple up on the ski-lift again and motioned his head for the other bears to look up.

"What are they up to?" Dave asked.

The bears seemed to be huddling together as if they were plotting something. That is *the* most unusual behavior for bears.

"Don't worry, they'll never get us up here," Suzanne said.

Below, a bear reared-up and started spitting out wolves at rapid fire speed.

Dozens of rabid, snarling, insane-looking wolves flew toward Dave and Suzanne like bullets; a barrage of hair and teeth and glowing red eyes piercing the darkness. Dave and Suzanne screamed like women at a screening of *Paranormal Activity.*

Most of the wolves missed their target. Two or three slammed into the lift but hit the rail or part of the wire and fell to their demise, yelping. The bear mustn't have had very good aim, or was night blind.

Dave and Suzanne were tripping out in full panic mode. Dave spilled his drink on her lap while screaming, "WOLVES! FLYING FUCKING WOLVES ARE COMING

AT US! HOLY SHIT! " and she didn't even notice.

A wolf whizzed past Suzanne's head.

Dave spazzed out. "There are *WOLF-SPITTING BEARS* in goddamn Flagstaff, Arizona! In Arizona! *WHAT THE FUCK, DUDE?!"*

There were totally wolf-spitting bears in Flagstaff, Arizona.

A bear climbed over the wolf-spitting bear and put his head down with his paw, as if to say, "Let me show you how it's done." The bear lined up his sights, carefully, and unleashed a barrage of wolves from his gaping maw.

The first bear feigned respect and was admittedly a little hurt.

More glowing red eyes flew toward Dave and Suzanne out of the darkness. But this time, their aim was more precise and threatening.

One wolf missed its target, hitting the bottom slab of the metal chair and bouncing off, but that was pretty close. One latched on to Dave's arm and clenched as one whizzed past Suzanne's head. It grazed her and made off with a mouthful of blonde hair in its jaws. The wolf shook Dave's arm in its mouth like a rag doll. Dave screamed his head off.

Two wolves flew straight at Suzanne's breasts and latched on to each one. They bit hard. She shrieked.

One wolf's teeth pierced one of Suzanne's silicone implants. The wolf didn't like the taste and spit it out, which made it fall off the chair to its death.

Cold air crept into the deep wound in Suzanne's breast. Her first instinct was to cover it up with her hand, but she had to yank on the wolf attached to her other boob. She hit Dave in the face with the wolf and gave him a bloody nose. The wolf on Dave's arm let go and jumped on Suzanne.

"GET THEM OFF ME! GET THEM OFF ME! GET THEM OFF ME!" Suzanne yelled as the growling wolves bit into her flesh, tearing her breasts apart and scratching her face.

Dave looked at the wolves. They were a sick-looking gray color and appeared to be covered in a thick layer of bear saliva. They looked like they had just been born. Dave suddenly remembered that he was allergic to any mammal, and especially reactive to their saliva. Then a wad of bear spit hit him right in the face.

"DAVE! HELP ME FOR FUCKSAKES!"

Dave flipped out and tried rubbing the spit off his face with a moist hot towel.

(The kind you get in first class –*The Narrator*)

"DO SOMETHING!"

Dave felt a sneeze coming on.

"GET THEM OFF OF ME! THEY'RE TEARING MY TITS APART! HELP!" Suzanne screamed painfully.

He looked at Suzanne and sneezed a massive sneeze. The kind that feels like its going to make your eyeballs pop out.

Dave's snot hit one of the wolves so hard that it was startled into letting go of Suzanne. It turned to growl at Dave, ready to jump and attack. Then something happened and it yelped, as if it felt a sudden pain. This changed its attitude completely.

It yelped again. The other wolf heard this and stopped attacking Suzanne to see what was wrong with his brother.

Dozens of tiny, wormlike parasites were digging into its skin. The wolf saw one disappear completely into his body, and thought, *fuck this shit*. He jumped off the ski-lift, landed on one of the bears' heads below, and almost knocked it out.

Suzanne and Dave looked at the wolf, now squirming around in their laps. Close-up they could see the worms eating it alive.

"Are those fuckin' worms all over it?!" Suzanne said, holding her breasts. "They're killing the thing! Where the fuck did *those* come from?"

Dave was looking closely in fascination.

A worm turned its head towards Dave. It was red and translucent-looking, with a face full of pointed, twisting fangs. It looked at him as if to say, "Hello, Dave," and dove into the wolf's pelt, disappearing.

Dave was astonished and dumbfounded. "I think they're my brain parasites."

"EW, GROSS!!!!" Suzanne kicked the wolf off the ski-lift. It hit the same bear in the head, and the bear was knocked out.

Chapter Four

Dave was applying first aid to Suzanne's chest—a bunch of wadded tissues and Spongebob Squarepants band-aids.

Suzanne was flipping out. Her breasts were badly wolf-bitten and leaking saline. "Did any of those parasites get into my tits?! Did they!?"

"I don't know."

"Oh my god, what if they did? What am I going to do?!? What if they're going to start eating me alive from the inside?!"

Dave had a thought. "Hey, remember that episode of *Friends* where Monica got stung by a jellyfish on the beach? And Chandler had to pee on her because that was the only thing that would help?"

Suzanne shot an *I'm going to kill you* glance at Dave.

"OK, fine. It was just an idea. Go ahead and have crazy worms eating your breasts off, what do I care?"

"ALRIGHT, FINE!" Suzanne shouted, throwing up her hands. "PISS ON MY FUCKING BOOBS, YOU SICK BASTARD!"

Dave pissed all over her boobs. And yes, he felt like a sick bastard.

Hoping that did the trick, Suzanne and Dave opened a bottle of finely aged Russian vodka and started passing it back and forth to each other—guzzling it like it was a bottle of fresh mountain spring water.

Suzanne took a big swig of it and wiped her mouth.

"Where the hell do you keep getting all this stuff anyways, Dave?"

Dave sighed. He was finally going to have to tell the truth about what happened.

"It all started a few weeks ago on vacation in Mexico…"

Dave told a long-winded story about backpacking to this awesome Mayan temple he'd heard about. Some dude told him all this killer shit about there being a Lost City of Gold, killer kush weed, and probably the best fried pork stand around. He found the pork stand first and went into great detail how it was probably the best Mexican food he ever had.

Then he discovered some awesome buds just growing wild and was picking them when he was caught by a big scary Indian warrior. Dave described the guy to have a big, sharp, tooth necklace, war paint, a headdress… you know, all the normal savage Indian dress-style. It was no surprise.

But he was knocked out and dragged back to the Mayan temple. He deduced that the Indians were Mayans, the lost race of people he heard about in history class that he didn't give a fuck about. It was also pretty obvious when he saw a desk calendar on the wall that had a bunch of red Xs on the days leading up to the end of December, 2012.

The Mayans were really mad at him for trying to take their weed, and the whole village beat him and fucked him in the mouth one by one, laughing, and ejaculating all over his face and down his throat. It seemed to go on for hours. It was the most horrifying thing ever. It was like *Deliverance* times fifty because in that movie, the fat guy was only raped by two people, and Dave had to give a hundred Mayans blowjobs.

"I've had this ability ever since. I just think of something I want, reach out and grab it, and there it is. As gross as it sounds, I think their cum was magic. When I got home I immediately got checked for AIDS and found out that I had brain parasites instead. I thought, *Okay, at least I don't have AIDS*, so thank god. And that's my whole flashback. What do you think?"

Dave looked at her expecting a big response, but she had passed out sometime during his long story. He'd wondered why he was getting to talk that much without being interrupted. He noticed the saline and piss on her boobs had frozen solid, which was good because it stopped the bleeding and would keep them stable until they could get down and go to the hospital. He put a big quilt over her and thought more about what happened to him in Mexico.

Down below, a bear had a flashback of spitting wolves at the people up on the ski-lift, couldn't remember what he was even doing in this area in the first place, and left. Then a wolf had a terrifying flashback of his friend being eaten alive by tiny worms and whimpered. The wolf looked back up at Dave, hoping he could somehow get revenge. But Dave didn't return the wolf's stare because Dave was too busy having a flashback of his flashback.

A deer was looking at the dead body of a wolf, pondering whether or not to eat the thing. It didn't look right. It was kind of sunken in with dozens of small red wounds that looked like bullet holes. But he'd seen a friend of his dead like that before and ate him and it was totally fine. The deer cursed himself for being so indecisive. He could never make a good choice! This was becoming a problem for him, since he already had enough self-esteem issues as it was.

On closer inspection, the wolf seemed to be moving. There was some kind of activity going on under the skin. The curious deer went in for a closer look.

A scary worm punched through the wolf's flesh and rose from its body. The deer froze. This was by far the biggest worm he'd ever seen. The worm opened its mouth to reveal a horrifying display of teeth and jumped straight at the deer, latching itself onto his face. The deer ran off screaming ,"OH MY GOD, OH MY GOD, I'M GOING TO DIE!" inside his head.

He stopped running when the worm ate through his head and started eating his brain. The last thought that went through the deer's mind was deep regret over making a horrible decision. Then he fell over and died.

Worms were squirming around all over the mountain, attacking and eating any prey they could find. They grew bigger and bigger, snatching owls out of trees, eating sign posts, and killing and destroying everything in their path.

Back in the deep jungles of Mexico, in an ancient Mayan tomb below the earth, a dark figure who looked centuries old suddenly opened his eyes.

And then he tore himself out of his own grave.

Chapter Five

The bears were back in the morning. The wolves too. It was just getting ridiculous.

Dave looked over the rail and saw them.

"Suzanne! Wake up!" he said, shaking her. "The bears are back! And the wolves too! This is just getting ridiculous."

Suzanne rubbed the salt from her eyes. "I thought that bears and shit mostly came out at night."

"Mostly? I dunno, I think bears come out whenever they want, but wolves come out at night mostly. And I guess wolf-spitting bears can come out any time they want, because they're different."

"I'm getting sick of this shit. We need to get off this mountain. We're going to die," Suzanne said.

"Yeah, well, we said that three days ago and we're still here."

"We might as well die. If we're ever saved I'm going to have to get my tits cut off." She looked down at her ravaged breasts. They were frozen solid with a mixture of blood, saline, and urine. She smelled like a human garbage can.

"Don't worry, you can get new tits. It's the future." Dave said, then sprayed a bit of air freshener on her boobs.

(It was potpourri. It smelled delightful. –*The Narrator*)

"They'll probably attack soon. Can't you get us something to defend ourselves with?"

"Wait a second, probably yeah."

Dave reached back and pulled out two giant medieval warrior shields, scabbards, and metal Viking hats with pointy horns on them. Those were his favorite kind of helmets. They just looked awesome.

Dave and Suzanne put them on, raised their shields, and readied their swords to fight the wolves. Which were going to fly at them from a bear's mouth and try to eat them alive.

The bears had a different plan this time. After another huddle, they walked over to the nearest pole and examined its ladder leading to the top of the lift.

A bear climbed onto another bear's back and stood up on his shoulders. The third bear climbed up that bear and the bear on the bottom stood up. The top bear could soon reach the bottom rung.

The bear started climbing up the ladder, much to Dave and Suzanne's horror.

While they were distracted with the astonishing site of a two ton black bear climbing up a ladder obviously too small for him, one of the bears below started spitting wolves again. Dave raised his shield just in time to block one of the snarling beasts from biting off his face. He was also suddenly worried he didn't have any brain parasites anymore. They were his secret weapon.

Suzanne cut a flying wolf in half. She decapitated another.

Dave chopped one up that landed in the chair.

While they were fighting flying wolves the bear checked out the cable holding the chairs. Then he shot several wolves at the cable. The wolves caught onto the wire and held on.

Meanwhile, the bear that climbed the ladder was chewing the mechanism that housed part of the cable on the top of the pole. He was biting and slashing at it. Dave heard the terrible sounds of grinding metal as the ski-lift chair rocked side-to-side violently. Grabbing onto Suzanne, he looked up to see what was going on. It appeared as though several wolves were coming at them on the wire cables hand over hand, legs dangling in the air as they panted heavily. Beyond that, Dave could see the bear causing all the destruction. Suzanne screamed when she looked behind them, as more wolves were climbing the wires on the other side towards them too.

(That's pretty fucked-up. *–The Narrator*)

The entire mountain started shaking.

"Earthquake!" shouted Dave.

Everyone held on for dear life. This included the wolves on the cables. The bear stopped chewing on the wire for a second and held on too. The rumbling stopped. Then one of the wires snapped and a whole line of terrified wolves went down with it, one by one. The ski-lift chair creaked and tilted to its side. Dave fell into Suzanne's arms. A wolf fell into Dave's.

An inhuman roar echoed from the top of the mountain, followed by a gigantic fiery explosion that sent fireballs flying in every direction. A behemoth-sized worm shot out from the peak, rising straight up with the flames, opening its gigantic maw.

Dave held on tight to the wolf in his arms as it buried its face in his jacket and whimpered. Dave sneezed all over it.

The rising worm, whose body seemed to be endless, fell forward onto the slope. An enormous thud shook the mountain to its core. Snow and trees went flying in every direction. The ski-lift operating booth exploded. The ski-lift poles fell over one by one. An avalanche rushed down the mountain with a gigantic worm on top of it. The huge worm roared as it surfed down the mountain toward them.

Everyone screamed.

The cable holding the occupied ski-lift chair finally snapped.

"HOLD ON!" screamed Dave.

They held on to the rail as tight as they could as the chair plummeted to the ground below. The wolf in Dave's arms covered his eyes.

The ski-lift chair landed upright in the snow, spun around backward, and slid down the mountain like some kind of hell ride. Dave and Suzanne screamed as a giant bear tumbled past them. A horde of wolves and the two other bears ran to catch up and escape the horror of the exploding mountain. One bear motioned his head toward the other, as if to say, *"Their fault!"*, and started spitting wolves at Dave and Suzanne.

They did their best to defend themselves as they rocketed down the ski slope backward in their out of control ski-lift chair, being chased by wolves that were running with bears, who were spitting wolves—all followed by a giant, screaming death worm, who was on fire and riding an avalanche down the mountain.

The chair took a sudden turn onto a side trail and slid to the bottom, where it came to a grinding halt by smashing into a tree. Dave and Suzanne flew through the air and landed on their faces in a snowbank.

Suzanne lifted up her head and saw that she was right beside the horribly worm-eaten corpse of a deer. She screamed.

Dave stood up and noticed he still held the wolf in his arms. He dropped it and went to help Suzanne. The wolf growled at him, and he kicked it in the face. It ran away whimpering.

Dave and Suzanne looked up to see the gigantic worm passing by them on the mountain. Its huge, red, worm-banded body went by, and went by, and kept going by…

"It must be over a mile long!" Dave yelled.

"HOLY SHIT!" Suzanne exclaimed, holding onto her boobs.

Then the three bears caught up to them and started circling the couple. One bear was covered in wolves and on fire. It went, "*GRRRRRR!*"

In a small pub nestled at the bottom of the mountain, a group of hippies in flannel t-shirts were sitting around a table drinking microbrews and smoking. Early '90s grunge blared on the stereo, and a hippie with dreadlocks was engaged in a furious debate with a hippie with probably too many piercings on his face. A second after he stood up and screamed, "Kurt Cobain was NOT a cum-guzzling faggot!", the giant worm barreled through the pub, obliterating it and killing everyone in an instant.

"What the fuck are we going to do now, Dave?" said Suzanne, suddenly wearing a dirty, gray tank top and camouflage pants.

"I don't know, dude. This might finally be it."

The bears slowly moved in for the kill. The lead bear opened its mouth wide and a slime-covered wolf's head popped out of it like it was being born. The wolf opened its mouth and snarled, showing off a face full of teeth.

Dave shuddered, weak in the knees.

Then all of a sudden, several anaconda-sized worms appeared from out of the forest and took the animals by storm. One in a tree lashed out at a bear, grabbed it, and took it into the trees kicking and screaming. Several other worms were gobbling up wolves like Hungry Hungry Hippos, except like worms. A worm bit off a bear's head, swallowed, bit off half its torso, swallowed, and gobbled up the rest.

Dave and Suzanne were already way the fuck out of there. They started running for it the second the shit started going down. They stopped at the top of a cliff overlooking the entire town of Flagstaff.

"Holy shit!" gasped Dave.

Flagstaff was a small and popular mountain town in Arizona. A big part of it was the college campus of NAU (Northern Arizona University) and was home to probably the biggest population of stoners in the whole state. The town was a nice destination for Phoenicians that liked to escape the heat and see the snow for once. It was notorious for its good breweries, vintage shopping district, and classic theaters. And it was being ripped to pieces by a gigantic death worm.

Part 2

Chapter Six

"Ramón, you have a telephone call."

"From who?"

"Didn't say."

Ramón sighed, put the last plate in the dishwasher, and turned it on. He took off his rubber gloves and went to the restaurant's office to answer the phone.

"Ramón here."

A creepy old voice spoke to him from the other line.

"It has begun. Alert the others. You know what to do."

Ramón tore off his hairnet. "Understood."

"Fiesta or death."

"FIESTA OR DEATH!"

Ramón hung up the phone and marched out of the downtown Phoenix restaurant, standing tall. He power-walked home like a man on a mission.

Ramón arrived home to his nagging wife and crying newborn.

He had one word for them. "Leave."

Seems like his wife understood, since she grabbed the car keys and was peeling out on the road in about ten seconds.

Ramón went into the bedroom and slammed the door. He got on his cell phone and sent a very urgent text message to eleven others. Then he went into the closet and opened up a chest that was buried beneath piles of clothes. He removed his katana from it and his black garb, which was folded neatly.

He got dressed and slung the katana over his back. Then Ramón took his poncho out of the hall closet, put it on, and disappeared with a flash into thin air.

Dave had Suzanne by the hand, and ran down the mountain with her into town. "OK, first we got to get back to my dorm and grab my iPod. I can't live without that. And then we've got to get you to the hospital."

"Fuck your iPod, my tits are melting!"

Dave looked at her tits. The frozen pee that was holding the wounds together was making her dirty tank top urine stained.

"Okay, okay I might know of a place we can stop on the way. But I'll be damned if I'm losing that iPod after all the work I've put into it."

(Dave spent weeks putting all his CDs back on it after it needed to be restored. He never wanted to do that again. It really sucked. –*The Narrator*)

There was a big explosion in the center of town. Then the mountain shook again.

Suzanne screamed, "WORMQUAKE!"

They held each other. Dave looked back at the mountain. Several more large worms were descending from it.

Dave grabbed her by the hand again. "Come on. We've got to go. NOW!"

They ran toward town.

The giant worm left a path of decimation through the center of Flagstaff. A big part of a historic avenue was completely destroyed. A drunk driving college student tried to take that way home but was stopped by a policeman for going the wrong way down a one way street. He'd get a DUI for sure.

He screamed, "FUCK!!!"

The worm stood up, towering a hundred feet in the air. It screeched, slammed into the ground head-first, and burrowed into the city. All of downtown flew up in the air completely detached from the Earth below and fell to the ground broken in pieces, completely wrecked, on fire, and exploding. Except for Flagstaff Brewery, which landed on the hill beside the observatory, completely intact. Everyone drinking there was totally fine and went out on the patio to smoke and watch the show. The owner decided to give everyone free beer and food for the rest of the night. The patrons went, "WHOOO!!"

The worm re-emerged underneath the local Barnes & Noble, mouth wide open, and swallowed the bookstore whole. Then it rose up and puked the entire place up all over the street. An acid-covered copy of "I'm Better Than You" by Helen Keller hit an old lady across the face, ironically blinding her. Then it flopped into the gutter where it belonged.

The worm headed toward the NAU campus, screeching and puking everywhere. People were screaming and trying to run away, and they were all mowed down in the worm's path.

A professor was teaching rocket Science to a group of mentally challenged young adults. He didn't understand any of what he was teaching himself, but the students were eating it up and getting it all. They were working on an exciting project to create a device that would take your entire iTunes library off your iPod and put it back onto your computer. Only they were able to understand the complex programming. They were so excited. The professor smiled and turned back to his chalkboard, so glad his class of mentally challenged students was pulling together so well.

Then the giant worm tore off the roof of the building and swallowed all the students whole. The Professor turned and screamed as the worm started spitting them out at him. He ran as his students' bodies flew all around him, hitting the ground and splattering everywhere. The Professor stopped when he noticed the upper torso of one of his best students, Tommy, reaching his hand out at him.

"Professor! Help me!" he screamed.

Then the Professor was decapitated by a flying retard.

"Stop! We've got to stop!" demanded Suzanne.

"What's wrong?"

"I don't feel so good."

Dave looked at her. Trickles of blood were coming out of her eyes, nose, mouth, and ears.

"You must have gotten some of my parasites inside of you!"

"What?! NOOOOOOO!!!!" Suzanne started punching him.

He blocked her with his arms. She seemed a little stronger than before.

"Get me to a fucking doctor, you bastard!" Suzanne yelled.

"OK, we'll go to my friend LeAnn's office, it's nearby."

"Is she a doctor?"

"Well, close enough. She's a veterinarian."

Dave expected a screaming mad response and more punching for suggesting an animal doctor check her out, but instead, Suzanne said, "Oh, I saw that in a movie once. That should be totally fine."

"Awesome!" Dave said and grabbed her by the hand and started running.

Up in the forest, a tall figure with long white hair and a flowing black cape was watching them. He followed, keeping his distance.

Several large differently colored worms descended upon the Flagstaff observatory and began a chaotic attack on the patrons of the relocated brewery. Drunk hippies and college students stumbled around screaming. Some were being eaten whole, some piece by piece, and some were smashed to bits by flailing worm tails.

The biggest worm shot through the brewery devouring all the beer vats in a line one by one. The stunned owner could almost see them exploding through the worm's opaque, green-skin. Then it reared up and puked, which created a beer tsunami that washed everyone off the side of the cliff, including all of the other worms.

"There seems to be a big worm inside her," said Dr. Romans, looking at a catscan. A dog barked in the next room, sequestered there because Dave was allergic to dogs too.

"What?!?! Are you fucking kidding me?" screamed Suzanne.

"BE QUIET!" shushed Dave. "LeAnn, go on."

"It seems as if the worm has replaced all of her vital organs. It might be the only thing that's keeping her alive right now."

"She's right," said a dark figure, who was there all of a sudden looking over them all.

Dave and LeAnn turned around and gasped.

"If you remove the worm it will kill her."

"Who the fuck are you?!" Dave shouted.

"Christ, I almost pissed myself, dude!" LeAnn said, checking her pants to see if they were dry.

The tall, dark man removed his cape and let down his long white hair. It set off a nice contrast with his brown skin.

The man shimmered like a source of light. "Allow me to introduce myself. I am Ponce De Leon II: The Revenge. Now listen to me, I know what to do and there isn't much time."

A white cat ran across the room in front of him.

(A white cat crossing your path is GOOD luck. *–The Narrator*)

Ponce went over to Suzanne and waved his magic hand, putting her to sleep. "She is important. We must get her to safety immediately. The Mexican Death Worm will be passing through this part of town any moment. None will survive."

Dave looked out the window and saw it coming. "And it looks like he's bringing friends."

Several other worms, almost as big, were right behind him.

"Do you know a safe place?" Ponce asked.

LeAnn spoke up, "My house, it's down the mountain in the next town near Sedona. It's about an hour away."

"Then the worms shouldn't have reached it yet," Dave said.

"Yeah, and I just called my husband. Everyone's totally fine. They're watching the whole thing on the news. I was about to get in my car and drive down there when you guys arrived."

"No," said Ponce. "The roads will not be safe."

He put his cape back on. "Now huddle around me my young amigos."

Ponce De Leon II: The Revenge whisked his cape around them, and they all disappeared in a flash of white light.

Seconds later the entire veterinary clinic exploded in a hail of shattered wood and glass. The giant worm passing through it went, "SCREEEEEEEEEEE!!!!"

The foursome reappeared in a flash of white light on the porch of Dr. LeAnn Romans' mountain aerie. Dave held Suzanne in his arms. She moaned. LeAnn swayed, almost falling over. Ponce caught her.

"The time-space-dimensional jaunt is very disorienting at first. But only for women."

LeAnn ran over to the porch railing and puked over the side.

Ponce whispered to Dave. "I know that sounds sexist, but sadly, it is true, mi amigo."

Dave figured it had something to do with ovaries or whatever and put Suzanne down on a lawn chair. He looked up at Ponce De Leon II: The Revenge. "Can you save her? And also, where the fuck did you come from and what the hell is going on?!"

"These are many questions, my friend. And there are many answers. I will reveal the answers to these questions and more. But not until the next chapter…"

Chapter Seven

"…of this dangerous adventure. We must reach the Mystical Sun City of the Phoenix and meet up with my companions. And then all will be revealed."

"You mean Phoenix?" asked Dave.

"If that's what they're calling it, then yes."

"But I live in Scottsdale."

"Scottsdale, Phoenix, same difference. Now about your girlfriend…"

"She's not my girlfriend."

"It does not matter, for she is already bonded to you from the source of the worms. And that source was you. She will undergo a terrifying transformation. LeAnn!" Ponce De Leon II snapped his fingers. LeAnn looked up, suddenly alert, and wiped the vomit from her mouth. "Fetch us all of your tequila, post haste!"

"I don't think I have any tequila in the house…"

Then her husband, Scott, opened the sliding glass door and yelled, "LeAnn, get your ass in here! We're having a margarita party! WHOOO!"

Ponce looked at her again and smiled. "And be sure to get some salt and limes."

Suzanne awoke from her enchanted slumber. She looked up and saw Ponce, Dave, LeAnn, and Scott looking down at her.

Ponce yelled, "Now, everyone! Hold her down!"

They all grabbed her and held her down. She started kicking and screaming.

"WHAT THE FUCK?!?! GET OFF OF ME YOU MOTHERFUCKERS!"

Suzanne spit up some blood and even more was trickling out of her eyes, nose, and ears.

Ponce De Leon II: The Revenge took some lime wedges and squeezed them in her eyes. She screamed in pain. When she was able to open her eyes again, Ponce threw a handful of margarita salt in them. She shrieked.

"Now! The tequila! Give me the bottle of tequila!"

LeAnn handed it to him.

"Is this guy going to like, buy us more or what?" her husband asked.

LeAnn shrugged.

Ponce opened the bottle and started pouring it all over Suzanne's face, making sure to get plenty of it in her eyes, up her nose, and down her throat. Suzanne gagged, gasped for air, and started convulsing all over.

"Yes! It is working!" yelled Ponce.

"Yes! WHOOO!! Thank fucking god, dude!" shouted Dave.

(Dave had no idea what was going on, but this was all still pretty exciting nonetheless. *–The Narrator*)

Then Suzanne's eyes rolled back in her head then popped out of her face. An eyeball landed in Scott's margarita glass, and not noticing, he took a sip. Then he saw it and went, "Ergwh!" and threw the glass down on the floor where it shattered.

"What the fuck is going on?!?!" screamed Dave.

"Just wait, you will see. JUST. KEEP. HOLDING. HER. DOWN!"

A round necklace of teeth appeared around her neck, biting deep into the skin, causing blood to bubble to the surface. The teeth climbed, biting. They revealed a bright blue, leathery tube of flesh emerging from the base of her neck. A thick, head-sized blue worm slowly ate her entire head, swallowing it whole, inch by inch, until it was gone.

A big blue worm head with a gaping round mouth full of sharp, jagged teeth writhed and snapped where Suzanne's head used to be.

Suzanne stood up, screeched, and spit her decapitated head through the window. It stuck in LeAnn and Scott's big-screen TV, shattering it. The children looked up and saw a blonde girl's head sticking out of their broken television and screamed. They ran away before the whole thing exploded.

Dave passed out.

Ponce yelled, "Grab her! We must wrap her in the mystical shroud of my people!"

The mystical shroud of Ponce De Leon II's people was a brightly colored fabric quilt featuring artwork of a sunbathing couple on a beach, enjoying a bucket of Corona beers.

"Hey! That's my blanket!" yelled Scott.

Suzanne screeched and ran. But she slammed straight into a wooden post and fell down backwards, since she was now a worm-head girl and had no eyes to see.

Everyone decided silently right there and then to call her Worm-Head Girl from then on.

LeAnn, Scott and Ponce tried wrapping the quilt around Worm-Head Girl as she rolled on the ground. It looked like they were trying to put out a fire. Which would've been a bad idea, since all the blankets from Mexico are extremely flammable.

"This guy's buying us a new TV, right?" Scott said to LeAnn.

"He goddamn well better."

They got Worm-Head Girl wrapped tightly in the shroud and Ponce De Leon II: The Revenge slung her over his shoulder. He kicked Dave in the ribs to wake him up.

"Come Dave! We must fly!"

"HEY!" shouted LeAnn, "You're not going anywhere until you pay for the goddamn mess you've made!"

45

"Yeah! And get us more booze!" Scott said.

Dave stood up, all groggy. Ponce hit him on the shoulder. "Dave! Take care of these people!"

Dave knew what he meant.

"Okay," he said and pulled out a cooler filled with dozens and dozens of tiny floating bottles of tequila and bottles of beer. LeAnn and Scott looked inside to see that each bottle of beer was stuffed with a hundred dollar bill. They jumped up and down in utter happiness.

"Thanks, LeAnn. You rule," said Dave.

Then Ponce De Leon II: The Revenge slung Dave over his other shoulder, ran off the patio, and took flight. LeAnn and Scott waved at him as he flew away.

Dave waved back, then remembered he left his iPod back in his dorm room, and screamed.

The I-17 South Freeway running out of Flagstaff was gridlocked in traffic. It was nothing but a big line of honking cars and panicking people going down the mountain. A big shadow loomed behind the traffic.

People turned back to see the giant doom worm barreling straight down the freeway. Everyone got out of their cars and ran away screaming. But it was futile. The Gigantic Mexican Death Worm slid down the freeway with its mouth wide open, gobbling up every car and fleeing human in its path toward downtown Phoenix.

Chapter Eight

Ponce De Leon II: The Revenge, Dave, and Worm-Head Girl came out of the sky and landed on the summit of Squaw Peak Mountain, a National Park and hiking destination in South Scottsdale that was named after the vaginas of Native American women.

Twelve men in ninja outfits were waiting for them. They stood in a perfect circle around the peak of the mountain.

"NINJAS!" said Dave, all excited, as he stepped down off of Ponce, running up to one. "Are you guys from Japan?! I'm the biggest kung-fu movie nerd ever! Oh my god, can you fly?!"

Ramón, the lead ninja, stared him down. "We are not the ninjas of your Asian sword and sorcery fantasy films!" he said, and tore off his mask to reveal his round eyes, brown skin, and perfectly trimmed black moustache. "We are MEXICAN Ninjas!" he exclaimed proudly.

The Mexican Ninjas all let out their war cry.

(It went, "AIE-AIE-AIE-AIE-AIE-AIE-AIE, AIE-AIE!" –*The Narrator*)

"Oh, sorry, I didn't mean to sound racist or anything." Dave said.

"Do not worry, young Dave. No offense taken." Ramón said. He got up close to Dave and whispered, "And yes, we CAN fly." Ramón winked at him.

Dave smiled gleefully.

Ponce De Leon II: The Revenge walked up behind Dave and put his hand on his shoulder. He stood next to him and said, "Yes, and that's not ALL my army of Mexican Ninjas can do. Just wait and see, they are going to blow your mind,

47

my young friend."

Dave just kept smiling like a gleaming idiot, and then suddenly remembered something. "Hey, I thought you were going to give me an explanation about what was going on?"

"Yes, in all due time."

Dave frowned.

"...Which is now!"

Ponce laid his cape down on the ground and sat down with Dave and started telling him the whole story.

"It began a long, long time ago, when my father, Ponce De Leon I: The First Offense, discovered the Fountain of Youth deep in the jungles of what you now call, 'Mexico.' But the ancient race of indigenous people—the Mayans—were protecting it. So, after my father killed them all and cut their fucking heads off, he and his men took off their clothes and went skinny-dipping in the lake of the Fountain of Youth and partied, thus becoming IMMORTAL!"

"WOW!!" Dave said, wide-eyed.

"I know, isn't it awesome?" Ponce smiled.

"So anyways, the remaining Mayans came up with this hairbrained scheme to convince everyone the world was going to end in the year 2012. But that was really just because they got really drunk and were too lazy to finish making up their calendar, and one of them had the idea that they should tell everyone that means something very foreboding instead. Then they raided my father's camp and stole all of the booze and raped and killed one of my father's favorite prostitutes, Melinda Etheridge."

"HOLY SHIT!"

"Yeah!" Ponce shouted.

"But the prostitute was ALSO my mother," he continued, "and my father was so heartbroken he decided to kill himself by eating one of the Forbidden Pigs of Mictlantecuhtli! His body burst with worms, which grew larger and larger, killing everything, and eventually chasing us all out of the Fountain of Youth forever!"

"OH MY GOD!"

"Yeah," Ponce said. "So, we all scattered and regrouped. And snuck back into the Mayan's camp to steal their secret recipe for a new kind of alcohol, called TEQUILA!"

"OOOOH!!!"

"Yeah. It is good."

"So after that, we defeated the worms and took back the Fountain of Youth where I plotted my revenge on the Mayan people. I was the new leader of my people. I sent my men into the Northern Country to settle and raise generations of warriors, in preparation for the chance that the day may come when the Great Worm rises again!"

"That would be us, amigo," said a Mexican ninja to Dave, pointing the tip of his sombrero at him.

Dave smiled.

"So, a few years ago," continued Ponce, "I wandered back into the Mayan temple to see if their ancestors had caught a whiff of the whole stupid Twenty-Twelve thing, and it turned out they did, since they had television and everything. It was all anyone was talking about, 'The end of the world' blah blah blah, 'The end of the Mayan calendar', blah blah blah. The stupid Mayans didn't even know anything about that until they heard about it on TV. They even watched the movie they made about it, *2012*, on bootleg, to get ideas, but they didn't like it so they tried to come up with another plan to end the world like was apparently predicted."

"Then they went into their ancestor's tomb and found the old Mayan calendar crumpled up and laying in the corner. They got all excited and went out immediately to the local Wal-mart and bought a new desk calendar, for the year twenty twelve."

"Oooh, I saw that! I was there!" Dave said.

"Yeah, okay. I know. But stop interrupting. Anyways, the Mayans also found little packets of dried eggs in the tomb, with directions on them that said, 'Add to Pork, Then Eat Pork, And Make Gigantic Death Worms.' They also saw a kid's painting on the wall of a giant worm eating the sun and were sure this was going to end the world. I tried to stop them, but they caught me, forced me to give them all blow jobs, and imprisoned me in their ancient tomb."

"Hey, that happened to me too when I was there. It was awful! But wait, don't you have a bunch of magical powers? Why didn't you stop them?" Dave asked.

Ponce looked at him dumbfounded for a second. "Anyways, moving on, they opened a fried pork stand outside near the temple, and that's when you came along and ate a burrito, thus contracting the worms, which you called 'brain parasites.' And I watched while you were being raped with my inner-eye and telepathically reached out and gave you a portion of my power."

"You mean the thing I can do, where I can pull whatever I imagine out of thin air?"

"Yes, that's the one. I knew I would need you to have it when the day came."

"So, I could probably get my iPod back right now if I wanted to, right?"

"Yes, just focus on where you left it and grab it."

Dave closed his eyes and saw it lying underground beneath a pile of rubble. But it looked intact, so he reached out and grabbed it.

"YEAH!" he exclaimed, "I GOT IT!"

"Good, young man! You have learned well. Now let me tell you how this is all going to fit into my plan…"

"Hold on, can you just wait a minute? I haven't heard any of my music in about a week now, alright? Can we just take a break?"

"This is an urgent matter…"

"Well hey, do you want my help or not? I just want fifteen minutes with my iPod, is that too much to ask?"

Ponce De Leon II: The Revenge pondered this for a second.

"Well, I guess it would be alright. But just fifteen minutes and not a minute more!"

"Sweet! I'm going to put on some old school death

metal!"

(Dave lied. He really put on the album, "Suddenly", by '80s pop singer Billy Ocean. *–The Narrator*)

"Okay," Dave said, returning to the group. He turned off his iPod and put it in his jacket. "Just how do I fit in?"

Ramón answered, "We need you to give us a nearly endless supply of tequila."

"You guys are going to get drunk the whole time?"

"No, not until we have defeated the enemy. Then we will have a huge FIESTA!"

"Fiesta or death!" one of them shouted.

"FIESTA OR DEATH!" they all screamed in unison.

"So, how are you guys going to defeat a bunch of giant death worms with a bunch of tequila?" Dave asked.

Ramón put his hands on Dave's shoulders and looked him in the eye. "All in due time, mi amigo. We just need you to do your part." Ramón smiled.

"Uh, okay. Any particular tequila you had in mind?"

"Nothing American."

"Gotcha."

Dave looked over to Suzanne, who seemed to be waking up from her slumber. Ponce De Leon II: The Revenge was helping her up.

"What about Worm-Head Girl?" he asked Ponce. "Where does she fit into all of this?"

"She is the backup plan. If all goes wrong, she may be able to form a telepathic rapport with the worms. Then it will be up to you to guide her."

A Mexican Ninja opened a chest full of bandoliers with holsters on them and started handing them out to the team. They all put them on.

"Now, Dave. The tequila." Ponce commanded.

"And NO WORMS in the bottles!" shouted Ramón.

Dave thought really hard about the slummiest, dirtiest

bar in all of Mexico, and found a couple cases of some local tequila. He checked to see if there were any worms at the bottom of the bottles. They were clear. He hefted and pulled them out one at a time.

The ninjas opened the cases, excited.

"Eh," one said, "this is the GOOD STUFF, VATO!"

"Perfect! You have done well, Dave." Ponce said.

The Mexican Ninjas put a bottle in each of their bandolier holsters.

Worm-Head Girl came up and tugged on Dave's shirt.

"What? Suzanne? Can you hear me? ARE YOU IN THERE?"

Suzanne's giant worm head nodded up and down.

"What does she want?" asked Ponce.

"I think, ERGH!" Dave said, holding his head like he suddenly got a big headache. "I think she's tapping into my brain with her mind. ERGH! It kind of hurts."

"Perfect! She is establishing a psychic connection with you in your brain, since part of her was born in there when she was one of your parasites."

"She's probably eaten lots and lots of your brain, you know." Ramón said.

"What is she saying?"

"I think she's saying she wants to help and wants weapons," Dave replied.

"What kind of weapons?"

"ERGH!! I… I think she wants a couple of handguns."

"Well, then. Get her the best handguns you can find in all of Arizona."

Dave reached into a local El Mirage pawn shop and got two awesome handguns, making sure they were loaded with bullets. "Here! Got 'em."

He handed them to Suzanne.

"Good choice, mi amigo! And with your psychic rapport you both should be able to…"

Worm-Head Girl turned around and shot Ponce De Leon II: The Revenge in the head. Then grabbed Dave and jumped off the mountain with him.

The Death Worms approached from the North. The main Giant Death Worm was now joined by several other Almost-As-Giant Death Worms on each side. They were all every different color you could think of.

The town of Anthem burst in flames as the worms barreled down the I-17 Freeway. The explosions could be seen from anywhere in the valley. The city went into full panic mode.

The worms were coming.

"The worms are coming!" screamed one of the ninjas.

The Mexican Ninjas unsheathed their katanas and went into action stances.

"Felipe, Marcos, stop the Worm-Headed Girl!" commanded Ramón. "Save Dave!"

"Si, señor."

Felipe and Marcos jumped off the cliff after them, throwing ninja stars at her as they flew down the mountain. She turned as she fell and started shooting up at them. Marcos flew away from the bullets, and Felipe blocked them with his iron wrist gauntlets.

Worm-Head Girl landed on a huge rock below and threw Dave down. She raised both of her handguns and continued shooting at the flying Mexican Ninjas.

They landed on either side of her, unwounded.

Felipe distracted her with a Mexican Hat Dance and then put his poncho on and turned invisible. Then Marcos took off his razor-edged throwing Sombrero and threw it at Worm-Head Girl while her back was turned to him.

"FIESTA OR DEATH!" he screamed.

She turned around to look and she was decapitated by the razor-edged throwing sombrero.

A fountain of blood from where her worm-head was shot up from her neck, splashing all over Dave, and covering Marcos and Felipe in a shower of blood.

"AIE-AIE-AIE-AIE-AIE-AIE-AIE!", they screamed and danced.

"WHAT THE FUCK, GUYS?!?! YOU KILLED HER!"

Marcos stopped, wiped the blood from his brow, and put his sombrero back on. "Well, I think anyone named 'Ponce De Leon II: The Revenge' would have wanted vengeance on the slug who took his life, ese!"

"But she was important! He said so! We needed her! And she was my friend!"

"Sorry, vato," Felipe said.

"Now get out of the way, we must get rid of the body."

Dave screamed, "NO! You're not going to throw her away like she's a piece of trash!"

While they were arguing, Suzanne rose from where she laid, headless, and came up behind Marcos and tapped him on the shoulder.

"WHA-?" Marcos replied, and he turned around to see No-Head Girl standing right behind him.

She grabbed him by the throat and started strangling him. Then a new giant blue worm head emerged from the hole where her old one had been, opened its mouth, screeched, and bit Marcos' head off.

(What was he thinking, anyway? Cutting a worm in half only makes new worms. Everyone knows that. *–The Narrator*)

Then Worm-Head Girl jumped off the rocks and ran away, shooting her guns in the air.

Ramón put Ponce De Leon II: The Revenge's cape over his dead body and then joined the others, who were standing on the edge of the mountain and watching the worms' progress.

"What is the progress on the approach of the Giant Death Worms?" he asked.

"Their arrival is imminent. They have reached Cave Creek."

Then, all of a sudden, all of the worms reared up, stood tall, and smashed face down into the earth, disappearing underground. The earth shook.

"Oh fuck," Ramón muttered.

"EVERYONE! Put on your ponchos. WE FLY!"

Felipe and Dave were nearly to the parking lot of Squaw Peak Mountain, in hot pursuit of Worm-Head Girl, when the earthquake started. They stopped and looked back to the summit.

"Everyone is still up there. Will they be OK?" Dave asked.

"Of course, they are the best of the best."

Then the mountain exploded in a fury of rock and dirt as a Giant Death Worm burst out of it, its giant mouth opening at the summit and screeching.

"HOLY SHIT!"

"Okay, they might all be dead."

Then Ramón and all the other Mexican Ninjas appeared out of thin air, taking off their invisibility ponchos.

"RAMÓN!" screamed Dave, running to hug him. "We thought you were dead."

"It will take a lot more than some crazy shit like that to kill ME, vato."

Dave smiled.

"Now, here is the plan…"

They all broke up into teams of two and all went flying in separate directions.

The Gigantic Death Worms started making Phoenix, Arizona nothing but a memory.

Part 3

Chapter Nine

"Welcome to 12 News at Five! I'm Mark Curtis," said Mark Curtis.

"And I'm Lin Sue Cooney," said his co-anchor, Lin Sue Cooney.

"Breaking news this evening, as what appear to be GIGANTIC DEATH WORMS, have come to Phoenix, and seem to be tearing the entire city to pieces."

"That's right, Mark. The Giant Worms are on a rampage, destroying everything, killing everyone, and altogether just causing mass destruction."

"And coincidentally, today is December twenty-first, twenty-twelve. Which marks the end of the Mayan Calendar," said Mark, smiling at the camera. "Looks like we have a virtual *End of Days* on our hands! Lin Sue?"

"Yes," she laughed. "It's the APOCALYPSE!"

"In other news," Mark continued, his big, gay mustache flapping, "Oscar-winning actress Lindsey Lohan has broken up with her beau, Sir George Clooney, and seems to be hitting the bottle again. Here's a picture of her naked at the recent…"

The newsroom exploded as the building was devoured by a Giant Death Worm.

(At the recent *what?!?! –The Narrator*)

Northwest of Phoenix in the town of Surprise, air raid sirens blared from Luke's Air Force Base. Everyone stopped sucking each other's dicks and fucking for a minute to see what was going on. Everything looked fine, so they went back to work.

The Air Force didn't have much to do since all wars had recently ended when America joined forces with France and gave everyone free gigantic statues for their countries. Everyone thought the gesture was so cool that they called a truce, since their gigantic statues were totally awesome.

So the military just laid around all day fucking and sucking, often high on meth and ecstasy. It was fair to say no one had joined the military in quite some time, since boot camp was about giving head and taking it up the ass.

A gigantic death worm barreled through the base, gobbling up all their killer war planes and crushing a bunch of army men in mid-orgasm. Then it reared up and slid all around town, shooting big death planes out of its mouth as ammunition, taking the town of Surprise by, well... surprise, really, when they saw a huge fucking worm spitting fighter jets out of its mouth.

Back at the base, the surviving soldiers, high as fuck on amphetamines, shrugged and then turned to necrophilia on their fallen comrades. After all, it's not GAY if you're DEAD.

At the Phoenix Zoo, the shadow of the worm descended on the park. The animals looked up at the sky when it blocked out the sun, which was very strange behavior for the animals because when there was ever a solar eclipse, they all knew better than to look at it.

The worm peered down at the zoo and started spitting out bears, wolves, deer, books, and beer. The animals tried to run away, but they were all in cages so they were pretty fucked. A flying bear landed in a bear cage and hit the wall, knocking it unconscious. One of the other bears went up to it to see if it was okay, and the bear stood up, growled, and started spitting wolves at him. Wolves clamped their jaws onto the bear's back, legs, and nose. He tried to shake them off but to no avail. The wolves ate him alive.

The other bears huddled together in the corner, shaking in fear as the wolf-spitting bear approached, growling at them. Then all of sudden they remembered they were bears, teamed up, and went and beat the shit out of him.

Lions jumped up to catch flying deer out of the air and went into a feeding frenzy. A pack of wolves landed head first into the crocodile swamp, and became tasty meals. A full library of books shot inside the chimp exhibit, and they all grabbed one and started reading. Then all of a sudden they got pissed off and started beating each other to death with them.

If worms could laugh, the Gigantic Death Worm was having a laugh riot. It started eating the entire place piece by piece.

Let this be a lesson about what happens when you cage animals. They will all get eaten by a Gigantic Death Worm.

In the town of Fountain Hills, which is basically a suburb of Scottsdale famous for having the World's Tallest Fountain and high concentration of meth addicts and pedophiles living upper class lifestyles, a giant worm was drinking from the fountain. The water shot up almost six hundred feet out of the middle of a big manmade lake. The worm looked like a kid at school drinking from the water fountain on a hot summer day. It even looked kind of happy, just lapping up water.

Of course, the entire town was flipping the fuck out, and running through the streets screaming.

Ramón and Dave flew in to the town and landed heroically at the historic and newly rebuilt Avenue of the Fountains, straight across from the fountain. Dave and Ramón looked up at the Giant Death Worm, which was splashing around the lake playfully.

"Aw, cute!" said Dave. "I always loved the fountain in winter time." He looked at Ramón and smiled. "I grew up out here, you know."

Then the Gigantic Death Worm noticed him. It screeched and came smashing down on the Avenue of the Fountains. It slithered straight at them.

(And you're going to die out here, you know. *–Han Solo*)

"Dave! Run! Distract it while I turn invisible!" Ramón commanded, quickly throwing on his poncho and becoming invisible.

Dave ran for his life and screamed while the Gigantic Death Worm barreled down the Avenue of the Fountains toward him.

Ramón tore off his poncho and unsheathed his katana sword as the worm passed him. He jumped and stabbed the side of the worm. He removed his sword and stabbed it higher into the worm, lightning fast. He climbed the worm that way, stabbing it over and over until he stood atop the monster worm.

The worm hadn't even seemed to notice.

Ramón thrust his katana deep into the worm's hide and cut a circular hole in it. Then he stabbed his blade into the center of the hole, and removed a big round piece of flesh like he was popping a cork. Ramón grabbed a tequila bottle off of his booze bandolier, carefully took off the cap, and then started drinking it.

After he slammed the entire bottle, he wiped his mouth and let out a sigh of refreshment. Then he had to steady himself because the worm was moving and shaking and barreling down the street, and he almost fell off the side. Ramón composed himself, then took the other bottle of tequila out of its holster in a flash, opened it, and jammed it bottoms up into the Gigantic Death Worm's brand new blowhole.

The worm screeched and slowed down as the entire bottle of tequila poured into its bloodstream. It tried to stop but had gained so much momentum chasing Dave that it just kept sliding down the avenue, screaming. Dave was backed against a wall. He had nowhere else to go. And he couldn't run off to the side because he was entranced by the Gigantic Death Worm coming straight at him screaming its head off.

I really am going to die out here, he thought.

But the worm, which looked huge coming down the street, was getting smaller and smaller somehow, shrinking by hundreds of tons as it barreled toward Dave. It stopped at Dave's feet looking like a harmless little earthworm. A bird flew down to snatch it up, and Ramón appeared from out of nowhere and stomped on the stupid fucking would-be thief.

Ramón grabbed the Miniscule Death Worm, which was crying and whimpering, and imprisoned it inside the empty bottle of tequila. He put the lid back on. "And that, mi amigo, is how we do it in MEXICO!"

Chapter Ten

(Chapter ten was deleted because it was nothing but a long-winded social commentary on the effects of brain parasites on human beings that became some kind of stupid analogy for third world suffering and contained some kind of complex political commentary on how you should fix all of the world's problems or else. It was boring as fuck, so it was thrown out completely. You're welcome. *–The Narrator*)

Chapter Eleven

Worm-Head Girl came home to find her mother passed out on the floor naked, face-down in a puddle of her own puke, which her dog was lapping up. As she entered the living room, she "saw" a family portrait of happier times—it was her, her mother, and her father, smiling happily over a cute new puppy with a huge bow on it. She raised her gun at it and shot the puppy in the face. The picture frame shattered and fell to the floor.

The dog started barking and her mother woke up.

She looked up at a filthy girl in camouflage pants and a dirty gray tank top, with a gigantic blue worm-head with a big mouth of grinding monster teeth.

"Suzanne?"

Worm-Head Girl screeched.

Her mother's boyfriend started slowly creeping up behind her from the bedroom, stark naked, with a golf club.

"ERGH!" shouted Dave painfully, holding his fingers to his temples.

"Dave! What is it?" Ramón said, slamming a shot glass down on the bar at the local authentic Mexican restaurant, Que Bueno.

"It's Suzanne."

"Worm-Head Girl?!"

"Yes, Worm-Head Girl! ERGH!" screamed Dave, obviously getting some sort of vision. "I think she's in trouble, Ramón. I think she's in trouble and needs our help."

"Do you know where she is?"

"Yes, she's in the biggest, most dangerous and disgusting cesspool in all of Arizona—Mesa."

"Then, mi amigo, LET US FLY!"

Ramón grabbed Dave and took to the sky with him. The Fountain Hills citizens cheered and called them heroes for saving their beautiful city.

Then another Gigantic Death Worm came from out of nowhere and landed on the townspeople, killing everyone instantly.

Worm-Head Girl's mom's boyfriend smacked her square in the back of her massive blue worm head with the golf club. She fell to the ground bleeding and screeching in pain. Then the dog attacked her and bit down on her arm, snarling. It dragged her over to her mother.

"YOU!!!" shouted her mother, pointing a finger of blame.

"I knew you had something to do with all of this, after what happened to Flagstaff. Look at you and your giant fucking worm head! You freak! YOU DISGUST ME!"

She kicked Worm-Head Girl in the ribs. Worm-Head Girl curled up into a ball. Her mom's boyfriend pulled her to her feet.

"And how could you let that happen to MIKE?!" he said, punching her in the stomach. "MY LITTLE BROTHER!!!" he punched her again, much harder. "YOU'RE GOING TO PAY FOR THAT!"

She shrieked.

He threw another punch at her, but this time Worm-Head Girl caught his fist in her mouth, swallowed his arm up to the elbow, and bit it off with a blood curdling screech.

He fell down screaming, blood shooting out of his stump like a firehose.

Her mother charged her, and Worm-Head Girl spit his

arm out at her. It hit her mother right in the face, knocking her out. She fell backward onto the dog, crushing it to death. It whimpered a death howl.

Then Worm-Head Girl took her pants down, and got on top of her mom's naked boyfriend, held him down and started raping him.

Dave and Ramón arrived at Suzanne's family home in a crime-ridden, decaying suburban neighborhood in East Mesa, to the sight of Worm-Head Girl raping a bleeding, screaming amputee to death. Worm-Head Girl shrieked in pleasure.

(And that's thanks in part to her victim having a very big penis, much unlike his little brother, whose dick was so small that she was totally fucking happy when he was killed. *–The Narrator*)

"Oh my god! It's so awful!" Dave said about the horrible scene.

"We should put him out of his misery, vato!" suggested Ramón.

"No, wait a minute, I'm getting pretty hard. Do you mind if we just watch for awhile? We could masturbate together, if you want." Dave suggested back.

"There is no way I am masturbating with a gringo to something as vile and disgusting as worm-rape!"

Ramón threw a knife at the poor guy, which killed him in the head. "Now, sometime after this is all over, I would not mind at all masturbating with you somewhere else, to something more sexually stimulating."

"Like a donkey show or something?"

"Yes, exactly." Ramón winked at him.

Then they turned to Worm-Head Girl, who was swallowing her mother's boyfriend whole. As he passed down her throat, there was a brief moment where his erection pressed out against her worm-cheek, giving the impression of Worm-Head Girl having a big dick in her mouth. And then it was gone.

"Suzanne!" screamed Dave.

Worm-Head Girl turned to Dave and Ramón with her handguns raised. A bullet awaited each of them.

"WORM-HEAD GIRL!" screamed Suzanne.

"No, your name is Suzanne. We go to college together in Flagstaff. Or, we used to. There's not much left of Flagstaff anymore. We were trapped on a ski-lift all week together. Your boyfriend, Mike, died. We were attacked by wolf-spitting bears. You contracted one of my brain parasites. I gave you cheeseburgers. You may look a lot different now. But you're still Suzanne."

Suzanne lowered her weapons. She looked at Dave, thinking for a minute.

"Worm-Head Girl... remembers."

Dave ran up and gave her a big hug. Ramón crossed his arms and smiled.

Then Suzanne's mother rose up behind her, holding a big chainsaw. She revved it up, held it over her head, and screamed.

They both turned around in quite a bit of shock.

(Especially because it seemed that Worm-Head Girl's mom just happens to have chainsaws lying around when she's drinking. But that's Mesa for you... —*The Narrator*)

Then a Gigantic Death Worm appeared behind Suzanne's mother, tore off the roof of the house, and bit her head off, then slammed down on top of her, smashing her to pieces, then gobbled up all the pieces, and spit them up, then ate them again, then spit up again to reveal a SHINY NEW RED BICYCLE!

"HOLY SHIT!" yelled Dave. "That's the same one I wanted when I was a kid! How did you know?"

"Worm-Head Girl... *knows*," she said caringly.

The giant worm stared at them both, licking its lips with its gigantic purple worm-tongue.

Ramón stepped forward. "It seems as though she has this worm under her control, just like the prophecy foretold."

Worm-Head Girl turned to him and said, "Worm *friend*!"

"Yes, Worm-Head Girl. Worm *friend*. That is so good right now!" Dave said, patting her on the head.

"It is the key to our victory." Roman stated, as if they'd already won. "Come, let us ride! We must reconvene with the others."

Ramón grabbed Dave and Worm-Head Girl, flew them to the top of the Gigantic Death Worm, and rode it into town.

"Aren't Mexican Ninjas totally fucking awesome?" Dave said.

Worm-Head Girl nodded.

All across Phoenix, teams of Mexican Ninjas defeated, shrunk, and bottled the Gigantic Death Worms. Fiesta was imminent. They all met up at Tempe Town Lake and awaited the arrival of their leader. The ninjas soon saw him arrive on top of the final Gigantic Death Worm. It slid into the lake, causing a tsunami that washed away most of ASU campus along with thousands of screaming students. The ninjas flew up to avoid this, meeting Ramón on top of the Gigantic Death Worm.

"Show me your bottles, compadres!" Ramón shouted.

The Mexican Ninjas raised their empty tequila bottles victoriously, and each and every one of them had a tiny death worm inside, shriveled up and dead.

"LET THE FIESTA BEGIN!"

"AIE-AIE-AIE-AIE-AIE-AIE-AIE-AIE-AIE!" they all screamed.

Dave pulled out an ice chest full of excellent imported beer, a few cases of good Mexican tequila, a grill with some hot dogs and hamburgers, some fireworks, a bunch of party hats, and some Hawaiian shirts for him and Suzanne. Worm-Head Girl looked lovely in hers.

Atop the worm, a fiesta to end all fiestas began. Phoenix burnt in all-consuming fire, lighting up the night sky romantically. Everyone danced. Dave pulled out his iPod, got a stereo for it, and appropriately blasted, "And We Danced," by The Hooters. Everyone drunkenly sang along to it. Later that night, he and Worm-Head Girl made love for the first time. It was awesome.

Nearby, Ramón beat-off furiously to their love making. When he came, it sprayed all over Dave's back. Startled, Dave and Worm-Head Girl looked up at him, and he ran away, embarrassed.

Dave smiled and then looked back down at Worm-Head Girl.

"Oh, *that Ramón!*"

She giggled, putting her arms around him.

They kept fucking all night to '80s R&B by artists such as Lionel Richie and Billy Ocean.

Chapter Twelve:
The Final Chapter

Dave and Worm-Head Girl woke up in the morning and packed up the empty bottles of tequila with the entombed death worms. Mexican Ninjas were cleaning up the trash from their fiesta by kicking it all off the side of the Great Last Worm.

Ramón walked up to Dave and gave him a hug goodbye. "You know what to do, my friend."

"I will miss you, mi amigo!" Dave cried.

"I will miss you too." Ramón looked over to Suzanne. "I will miss you as well, Worm-Head Girl."

"WORM-HEAD GIRL WILL MISS YOU TOO. WORM-HEAD GIRL SAD."

She went over and hugged Ramón. Ramón squeezed her ass.

"Take good care of him."

"WORM-HEAD GIRL TRY NOT TO EAT HIM. BUT WORM-HEAD GIRL PROMISES NOTHING."

"Okay, fair enough."

Then he flew up into the air and shouted, "Good luck, mi amigos!"

He met up with the other flying Mexican Ninjas, and they all flew away screaming, "AIE-AIE-AIE-AIE-AIE-AIE-AIE-AIE-AIE!"

"Next stop, Mexico," Dave told Suzanne.

She waved her arm and the Gigantic Death Worm snapped into action, worming its way south to the border, bulldozing over hundreds of survivors in makeshift hospital tents, and killing them all in its huge worm-ridden path.

Epilogue

Dave and Suzanne arrived at the Mayan Temple deep in the jungles of the Mexican, um, *jungles*. The Mayan people were lazing around, drinking tequila, smoking pot, and sucking each other off when the Gigantic Death Worm's head appeared over the trees. They all stood up and screamed.

One pointed and shouted, "LOOK! THE GRINGO RETURNS! HE'S COME TO BRING DEATH TO US ALL! RUN!"

Dave looked down at them victoriously and screamed, "HA-HA! GO BACK TO THE *WORMS!*"

He brought the Gigantic Death Worm down on them head first, mouth open, and it devoured the entire place and all of the Mayan people in an exploding fury of earth and stone.

The worm came to rest in the decimated village.

Dave shook his fist, smiled, and shouted, "NO FIESTA FOR YOU!" Worm-Head Girl tapped him on the shoulder to get his attention and then pointed at a gigantic gaping hole in the ground where the Mayan Temple once stood. "DOES DAVE SEE WHAT WORM-HEAD GIRL SEES?" she asked.

"No, it can't be…" Dave gasped. He hugged Worm-Head Girl and shook her excitedly. "WE'VE FOUND IT—*THE LOST CITY OF GOLD!*"

They both cheered and went over to the new McDonald's that suddenly appeared nearby to celebrate.

McDonald's is awesome.

Vince Kramer is a crazy person who won't hesitate to attack the X-Men in the morning, the Justice League in the afternoon, and have the entire cast of *Friends* raped and murdered by midnight. He also isn't real and a figment of your imagination. Actually, all of his works were really done by the Mothman. Having two head surgeries by the age of 18, he had one million Lite-Brite bulbs inserted into his brain. This makes him immortal. He lives in Happy Valley, Oregon, alone with his pet iguana, Desmond Harrington. He loves Desmond Harrington, cult horror films, G.I. Joe, death metal, the '80s, Star Wars, and Devo. He hates animal hair, the sun, midgets, politics, and transvestites. His greatest fear is being outside and having an allergy attack, while he's being raped by transvestites, as midgets stab him and talk his ear off about politics. He's also afraid of air. He thinks being a Conservative Republican is funny, even though he has no idea what it means. Sometimes, if you're lucky, you can see him power-walking through the Hollywood District in a full-on Star Trek: The Next Generation Captain's uniform, attacking homeless people with silly string. He loves you and wants your smell all over him.

BIZARRO BOOKS

CATALOG   FALL 2011

ERASERHEAD PRESS

Your major resource for the bizarro fiction genre:

WWW.BIZARROCENTRAL.COM

Introduce yourselves to the bizarro fiction genre and all of its authors with the Bizarro Starter Kit series. Each volume features short novels and short stories by ten of the leading bizarro authors, designed to give you a perfect sampling of the genre for only $10.

BB-0X1
"The Bizarro Starter Kit" (Orange)

Featuring D. Harlan Wilson, Carlton Mellick III, Jeremy Robert Johnson, Kevin L Donihe, Gina Ranalli, Andre Duza, Vincent W. Sakowski, Steve Beard, John Edward Lawson, and Bruce Taylor. **236 pages $10**

BB-0X2
"The Bizarro Starter Kit" (Blue)

Featuring Ray Fracalossy, Jeremy C. Shipp, Jordan Krall, Mykle Hansen, Andersen Prunty, Eckhard Gerdes, Bradley Sands, Steve Aylett, Christian TeBordo, and Tony Rauch. **244 pages $10**

BB-0X2
"The Bizarro Starter Kit" (Purple)

Featuring Russell Edson, Athena Villaverde, David Agranoff, Matthew Revert, Andrew Goldfarb, Jeff Burk, Garrett Cook, Kris Saknussemm, Cody Goodfellow, and Cameron Pierce **264 pages $10**

BB-001 **"The Kafka Effekt" D. Harlan Wilson** — A collection of forty-four irreal short stories loosely written in the vein of Franz Kafka, with more than a pinch of William S. Burroughs sprinkled on top. **211 pages $14**

BB-002 **"Satan Burger" Carlton Mellick III** — The cult novel that put Carlton Mellick III on the map ... Six punks get jobs at a fast food restaurant owned by the devil in a city violently overpopulated by surreal alien cultures. **236 pages $14**

BB-003 **"Some Things Are Better Left Unplugged" Vincent Sakwoski** — Join The Man and his Nemesis, the obese tabby, for a nightmare roller coaster ride into this postmodern fantasy. **152 pages $10**

BB-004 **"Shall We Gather At the Garden?" Kevin L Donihe** — Donihe's Debut novel. Midgets take over the world, The Church of Lionel Richie vs. The Church of the Byrds, plant porn and more! **244 pages $14**

BB-005 **"Razor Wire Pubic Hair" Carlton Mellick III** — A genderless humandildo is purchased by a razor dominatrix and brought into her nightmarish world of bizarre sex and mutilation. **176 pages $11**

BB-006 **"Stranger on the Loose" D. Harlan Wilson** — The fiction of Wilson's 2nd collection is planted in the soil of normalcy, but what grows out of that soil is a dark, witty, otherworldly jungle... **228 pages $14**

BB-007 **"The Baby Jesus Butt Plug" Carlton Mellick III** — Using clones of the Baby Jesus for anal sex will be the hip sex fetish of the future. **92 pages $10**

BB-008 **"Fishyfleshed" Carlton Mellick III** — The world of the past is an illogical flatland lacking in dimension and color, a sick-scape of crispy squid people wandering the desert for no apparent reason. **260 pages $14**

BB-009 **"Dead Bitch Army"** **Andre Duza** — Step into a world filled with racist teenagers, cannibals, 100 warped Uncle Sams, automobiles with razor-sharp teeth, living graffiti, and a pissed-off zombie bitch out for revenge. **344 pages** **$16**

BB-010 **"The Menstruating Mall"** **Carlton Mellick III** — "The Breakfast Club meets Chopping Mall as directed by David Lynch." - Brian Keene **212 pages** **$12**

BB-011 **"Angel Dust Apocalypse"** **Jeremy Robert Johnson** — Meth-heads, man-made monsters, and murderous Neo-Nazis. "Seriously amazing short stories..." - Chuck Palahniuk, author of Fight Club **184 pages** **$11**

BB-012 **"Ocean of Lard"** **Kevin L Donihe / Carlton Mellick III** — A parody of those old Choose Your Own Adventure kid's books about some very odd pirates sailing on a sea made of animal fat. **176 pages** **$12**

BB-015 **"Foop!"** **Chris Genoa** — Strange happenings are going on at Dactyl, Inc, the world's first and only time travel tourism company. "A surreal pie in the face!" - Christopher Moore **300 pages** **$14**

BB-020 **"Punk Land"** **Carlton Mellick III** — In the punk version of Heaven, the anarchist utopia is threatened by corporate fascism and only Goblin, Mortician's sperm, and a blue-mohawked female assassin named Shark Girl can stop them. **284 pages** **$15**

BB-027 **"Siren Promised"** **Jeremy Robert Johnson & Alan M Clark** — Nominated for the Bram Stoker Award. A potent mix of bad drugs, bad dreams, brutal bad guys, and surreal/incredible art by Alan M. Clark. **190 pages** **$13**

BB-031 **"Sea of the Patchwork Cats"** **Carlton Mellick III** — A quiet dreamlike tale set in the ashes of the human race. For Mellick enthusiasts who also adore The Twilight Zone. **112 pages** **$10**

BB-032 **"Extinction Journals" Jeremy Robert Johnson** — An uncanny voyage across a newly nuclear America where one man must confront the problems associated with loneliness, insane dieties, radiation, love, and an ever-evolving cockroach suit with a mind of its own. **104 pages $10**

BB-037 **"The Haunted Vagina" Carlton Mellick III** — It's difficult to love a woman whose vagina is a gateway to the world of the dead. **132 pages $10**

BB-043 **"War Slut" Carlton Mellick III** — Part "1984," part "Waiting for Godot," and part action horror video game adaptation of John Carpenter's "The Thing." **116 pages $10**

BB-047 **"Sausagey Santa" Carlton Mellick III** — A bizarro Christmas tale featuring Santa as a piratey mutant with a body made of sausages. 124 pages $10

BB-048 **"Misadventures in a Thumbnail Universe" Vincent Sakowski** — Dive deep into the surreal and satirical realms of neo-classical Blender Fiction, filled with television shoes and flesh-filled skies. **120 pages $10**

BB-053 **"Ballad of a Slow Poisoner" Andrew Goldfarb** — Millford Mutterwurst sat down on a Tuesday to take his afternoon tea, and made the unpleasant discovery that his elbows were becoming flatter. **128 pages $10**

BB-055 **"Help! A Bear is Eating Me" Mykle Hansen** — The bizarro, heartwarming, magical tale of poor planning, hubris and severe blood loss... **150 pages $11**

BB-056 **"Piecemeal June" Jordan Krall** — A man falls in love with a living sex doll, but with love comes danger when her creator comes after her with crab-squid assassins. **90 pages $9**

BB-058 **"The Overwhelming Urge" Andersen Prunty** — A collection of bizarro tales by Andersen Prunty. **150 pages $11**

BB-059 **"Adolf in Wonderland" Carlton Mellick III** — A dreamlike adventure that takes a young descendant of Adolf Hitler's design and sends him down the rabbit hole into a world of imperfection and disorder. **180 pages $11**

BB-061 **"Ultra Fuckers" Carlton Mellick III** — Absurdist suburban horror about a couple who enter an upper middle class gated community but can't find their way out. **108 pages $9**

BB-062 **"House of Houses" Kevin L. Donihe** — An odd man wants to marry his house. Unfortunately, all of the houses in the world collapse at the same time in the Great House Holocaust. Now he must travel to House Heaven to find his departed fiancee. **172 pages $11**

BB-064 **"Squid Pulp Blues" Jordan Krall** — In these three bizarro-noir novellas, the reader is thrown into a world of murderers, drugs made from squid parts, deformed gun-toting veterans, and a mischievous apocalyptic donkey. **204 pages $12**

BB-065 **"Jack and Mr. Grin" Andersen Prunty** — "When Mr. Grin calls you can hear a smile in his voice. Not a warm and friendly smile, but the kind that seizes your spine in fear. You don't need to pay your phone bill to hear it. That smile is in every line of Prunty's prose." - Tom Bradley. **208 pages $12**

BB-066 **"Cybernetrix" Carlton Mellick III** — What would you do if your normal everyday world was slowly mutating into the video game world from Tron? **212 pages $12**

BB-072 **"Zerostrata" Andersen Prunty** — Hansel Nothing lives in a tree house, suffers from memory loss, has a very eccentric family, and falls in love with a woman who runs naked through the woods every night. **144 pages $11**

BB-073 **"The Egg Man" Carlton Mellick III** — It is a world where humans reproduce like insects. Children are the property of corporations, and having an enormous ten-foot brain implanted into your skull is a grotesque sexual fetish. Mellick's industrial urban dystopia is one of his darkest and grittiest to date. **184 pages $11**

BB-074 **"Shark Hunting in Paradise Garden" Cameron Pierce** — A group of strange humanoid religious fanatics travel back in time to the Garden of Eden to discover it is invested with hundreds of giant flying maneating sharks. **150 pages $10**

BB-075 **"Apeshit" Carlton Mellick III** - Friday the 13th meets Visitor Q. Six hipster teens go to a cabin in the woods inhabited by a deformed killer. An incredibly fucked-up parody of B-horror movies with a bizarro slant. **192 pages $12**

BB-076 **"Fuckers of Everything on the Crazy Shitting Planet of the Vomit At smosphere" Mykle Hansen** - Three bizarro satires. Monster Cocks, Journey to the Center of Agnes Cuddlebottom, and Crazy Shitting Planet. **228 pages $12**

BB-077 **"The Kissing Bug" Daniel Scott Buck** — In the tradition of Roald Dahl, Tim Burton, and Edward Gorey, comes this bizarro anti-war children's story about a bohemian conenose kissing bug who falls in love with a human woman. **116 pages $10**

BB-078 **"MachoPoni" Lotus Rose** — It's My Little Pony... *Bizarro* style! A long time ago Poniworld was split in two. On one side of the Jagged Line is the Pastel Kingdom, a magical land of music, parties, and positivity. On the other side of the Jagged Line is Dark Kingdom inhabited by an army of undead ponies. **148 pages $11**

BB-079 **"The Faggiest Vampire" Carlton Mellick III** — A Roald Dahl-esque children's story about two faggy vampires who partake in a mustache competition to find out which one is truly the faggiest. **104 pages $10**

BB-080 **"Sky Tongues" Gina Ranalli** — The autobiography of Sky Tongues, the biracial hermaphrodite actress with tongues for fingers. Follow her strange life story as she rises from freak to fame. **204 pages $12**

BB-081 **"Washer Mouth" Kevin L. Donihe** - A washing machine becomes human and pursues his dream of meeting his favorite soap opera star. **244 pages $11**

BB-082 **"Shatnerquake" Jeff Burk** - All of the characters ever played by William Shatner are suddenly sucked into our world. Their mission: hunt down and destroy the real William Shatner. **100 pages $10**

BB-083 **"The Cannibals of Candyland" Carlton Mellick III** - There exists a race of cannibals that are made of candy. They live in an underground world made out of candy. One man has dedicated his life to killing them all. **170 pages $11**

BB-084 **"Slub Glub in the Weird World of the Weeping Willows"** **Andrew Goldfarb** - The charming tale of a blue glob named Slub Glub who helps the weeping willows whose tears are flooding the earth. There are also hyenas, ghosts, and a voodoo priest **100 pages $10**

BB-085 **"Super Fetus" Adam Pepper** - Try to abort this fetus and he'll kick your ass! **104 pages $10**

BB-086 **"Fistful of Feet" Jordan Krall** - A bizarro tribute to spaghetti westerns, featuring Cthulhu-worshipping Indians, a woman with four feet, a crazed gunman who is obsessed with sucking on candy, Syphilis-ridden mutants, sexually transmitted tattoos, and a house devoted to the freakiest fetishes. **228 pages $12**

BB-087 **"Ass Goblins of Auschwitz" Cameron Pierce** - It's Monty Python meets Nazi exploitation in a surreal nightmare as can only be imagined by Bizarro author Cameron Pierce. **104 pages $10**

BB-088 **"Silent Weapons for Quiet Wars" Cody Goodfellow** - "This is high-end psychological surrealist horror meets bottom-feeding low-life crime in a techno-thrilling science fiction world full of Lovecraft and magic..." -John Skipp **212 pages $12**

BB-089 "Warrior Wolf Women of the Wasteland" Carlton Mellick III
— Road Warrior Werewolves versus McDonaldland Mutants...post-apocalyptic fiction has never been quite like this. **316 pages $13**

BB-091 "Super Giant Monster Time" Jeff Burk — A tribute to choose your own adventures and Godzilla movies. Will you escape the giant monsters that are rampaging the fuck out of your city and shit? Or will you join the mob of alien-controlled punk rockers causing chaos in the streets? What happens next depends on you. **188 pages $12**

BB-092 "Perfect Union" Cody Goodfellow — "Cronenberg's THE FLY on a grand scale: human/insect gene-spliced body horror, where the human hive politics are as shocking as the gore." -John Skipp. **272 pages $13**

BB-093 "Sunset with a Beard" Carlton Mellick III — 14 stories of surreal science fiction. **200 pages $12**

BB-094 "My Fake War" Andersen Prunty — The absurd tale of an unlikely soldier forced to fight a war that, quite possibly, does not exist. It's Rambo meets Waiting for Godot in this subversive satire of American values and the scope of the human imagination. **128 pages $11**

BB-095 "Lost in Cat Brain Land" Cameron Pierce — Sad stories from a surreal world. A fascist mustache, the ghost of Franz Kafka, a desert inside a dead cat. Primordial entities mourn the death of their child. The desperate serve tea to mysterious creatures. A hopeless romantic falls in love with a pterodactyl. And much more. **152 pages $11**

BB-096 "The Kobold Wizard's Dildo of Enlightenment +2" Carlton Mellick III — A Dungeons and Dragons parody about a group of people who learn they are only made up characters in an AD&D campaign and must find a way to resist their nerdy teenaged players and retarded dungeon master in order to survive. 232 **pages $12**

BB-098 "A Hundred Horrible Sorrows of Ogner Stump" Andrew Goldfarb — Goldfarb's acclaimed comic series. A magical and weird journey into the horrors of everyday life. **164 pages $11**

BB-099 **"Pickled Apocalypse of Pancake Island" Cameron Pierce**—A demented fairy tale about a pickle, a pancake, and the apocalypse. **102 pages $8**

BB-100 **"Slag Attack" Andersen Prunty**— Slag Attack features four visceral, noir stories about the living, crawling apocalypse.A slag is what survivors are calling the slug-like maggots raining from the sky, burrowing inside people, and hollowing out their flesh and their sanity. **148 pages $11**

BB-101 **"Slaughterhouse High" Robert Devereaux**—A place where schools are built with secret passageways, rebellious teens get zippers installed in their mouths and genitals, and once a year, on that special night, one couple is slaughtered and the bits of their bodies are kept as souvenirs. **304 pages $13**

BB-102 **"The Emerald Burrito of Oz" John Skipp & Marc Levinthal** —OZ IS REAL! Magic is real! The gate is really in Kansas! And America is finally allowing Earth tourists to visit this weird-ass, mysterious land. But when Gene of Los Angeles heads off for summer vacation in the Emerald City, little does he know that a war is brewing...a war that could destroy both worlds. **280 pages $13**

BB-103 **"The Vegan Revolution... with Zombies" David Agranoff** — When there's no more meat in hell, the vegans will walk the earth. **160 pages $11**

BB-104 **"The Flappy Parts" Kevin L Donihe**—Poems about bunnies, LSD, and police abuse. You know, things that matter. 132 **pages $11**

BB-105 **"Sorry I Ruined Your Orgy" Bradley Sands**—Bizarro humorist Bradley Sands returns with one of the strangest, most hilarious collections of the year. **130 pages $11**

BB-106 **"Mr. Magic Realism" Bruce Taylor**—Like Golden Age science fiction comics written by Freud, *Mr. Magic Realism* is a strange, insightful adventure that spans the furthest reaches of the galaxy, exploring the hidden caverns in the hearts and minds of men, women, aliens, and biomechanical cats. **152 pages $11**

BB-107 **"Zombies and Shit" Carlton Mellick III**—"Battle Royale" meets "Return of the Living Dead." Mellick's bizarro tribute to the zombie genre. **308 pages $13**

BB-108 **"The Cannibal's Guide to Ethical Living" Mykle Hansen**— Over a five star French meal of fine wine, organic vegetables and human flesh, a lunatic delivers a witty, chilling, disturbingly sane argument in favor of eating the rich.. **184 pages $11**

BB-109 **"Starfish Girl" Athena Villaverde**—In a post-apocalyptic underwater dome society, a girl with a starfish growing from her head and an assassin with sea anenome hair are on the run from a gang of mutant fish men. **160 pages $11**

BB-110 **"Lick Your Neighbor" Chris Genoa**—Mutant ninjas, a talking whale, kung fu masters, maniacal pilgrims, and an alcoholic clown populate Chris Genoa's surreal, darkly comical and unnerving reimagining of the first Thanksgiving. **303 pages $13**

BB-111 **"Night of the Assholes" Kevin L. Donihe**—A plague of assholes is infecting the countryside. Normal everyday people are transforming into jerks, snobs, dicks, and douchebags. And they all have only one purpose: to make your life a living hell.. **192 pages $11**

BB-112 **"Jimmy Plush, Teddy Bear Detective" Garrett Cook**—Hardboiled cases of a private detective trapped within a teddy bear body. **180 pages $11**

BB-113 **"The Deadheart Shelters" Forrest Armstrong**—The hip hop lovechild of William Burroughs and Dali... **144 pages $11**

BB-114 **"Eyeballs Growing All Over Me... Again" Tony Raugh**— Absurd, surreal, playful, dream-like, whimsical, and a lot of fun to read. **144 pages $11**

BB-115 **"Whargoul" Dave Brockie** — From the killing grounds of Stalingrad to the death camps of the holocaust. From torture chambers in Iraq to race riots in the United States, the Whargoul was there, killing and raping. **244 pages $12**

BB-116 **"By the Time We Leave Here, We'll Be Friends" J. David Osborne** — A David Lynchian nightmare set in a Russian gulag, where its prisoners, guards, traitors, soldiers, lovers, and demons fight for survival and their own rapidly deteriorating humanity. **168 pages $11**

BB-117 **"Christmas on Crack" edited by Carlton Mellick III** — Perverted Christmas Tales for the whole family! . . . as long as every member of your family is over the age of 18. **168 pages $11**

BB-118 **"Crab Town" Carlton Mellick III** — Radiation fetishists, balloon people, mutant crabs, sail-bike road warriors, and a love affair between a woman and an H-Bomb. This is one mean asshole of a city. Welcome to Crab Town. **100 pages $8**

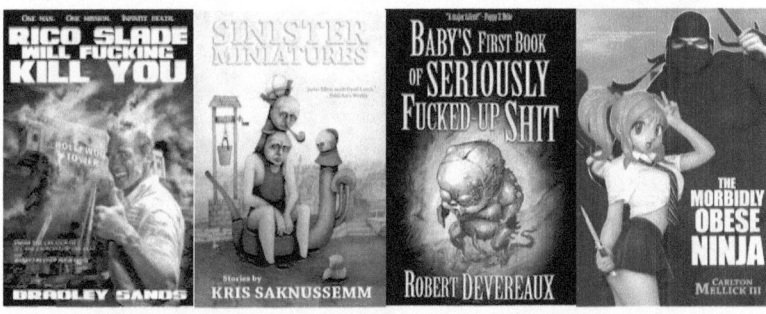

BB-119 **"Rico Slade Will Fucking Kill You" Bradley Sands** — Rico Slade is an action hero. Rico Slade can rip out a throat with his bare hands. Rico Slade's favorite food is the honey-roasted peanut. Rico Slade will fucking kill everyone. A novel. **122 pages $8**

BB-120 **"Sinister Miniatures" Kris Saknussemm** — The definitive collection of short fiction by Kris Saknussemm, confirming that he is one of the best, most daring writers of the weird to emerge in the twenty-first century. **180 pages $11**

BB-121 **"Baby's First Book of Seriously Fucked up Shit" Robert Devereaux** — Ten stories of the strange, the gross, and the just plain fucked up from one of the most original voices in horror. **176 pages $11**

BB-122 **"The Morbidly Obese Ninja" Carlton Mellick III** — These days, if you want to run a successful company . . . you're going to need a lot of ninjas. **92 pages $8**

BB-107 **"Zombies and Shit" Carlton Mellick III**—"Battle Royale" meets "Return of the Living Dead." Mellick's bizarro tribute to the zombie genre. **308 pages $13**

BB-108 **"The Cannibal's Guide to Ethical Living" Mykle Hansen**—Over a five star French meal of fine wine, organic vegetables and human flesh, a lunatic delivers a witty, chilling, disturbingly sane argument in favor of eating the rich.. **184 pages $11**

BB-109 **"Starfish Girl" Athena Villaverde**—In a post-apocalyptic underwater dome society, a girl with a starfish growing from her head and an assassin with sea anemone hair are on the run from a gang of mutant fish men. **160 pages $11**

BB-110 **"Lick Your Neighbor" Chris Genoa**—Mutant ninjas, a talking whale, kung fu masters, maniacal pilgrims, and an alcoholic clown populate Chris Genoa's surreal, darkly comical and unnerving reimagining of the first Thanksgiving. **303 pages $13**

BB-111 **"Night of the Assholes" Kevin L. Donihe**—A plague of assholes is infecting the countryside. Normal everyday people are transforming into jerks, snobs, dicks, and douchebags. And they all have only one purpose: to make your life a living hell.. **192 pages $11**

BB-112 **"Jimmy Plush, Teddy Bear Detective" Garrett Cook**—Hardboiled cases of a private detective trapped within a teddy bear body. **180 pages $11**

BB-113 **"The Deadheart Shelters" Forrest Armstrong**—The hip hop lovechild of William Burroughs and Dali... **144 pages $11**

BB-114 **"Eyeballs Growing All Over Me... Again" Tony Raugh**—Absurd, surreal, playful, dream-like, whimsical, and a lot of fun to read. **144 pages $11**

BB-115 "Whargoul" Dave Brockie — From the killing grounds of Stalingrad to the death camps of the holocaust. From torture chambers in Iraq to race riots in the United States, the Whargoul was there, killing and raping. **244 pages $12**

BB-116 "By the Time We Leave Here, We'll Be Friends" J. David Osborne — A David Lynchian nightmare set in a Russian gulag, where its prisoners, guards, traitors, soldiers, lovers, and demons fight for survival and their own rapidly deteriorating humanity. **168 pages $11**

BB-117 "Christmas on Crack" edited by Carlton Mellick III — Perverted Christmas Tales for the whole family! . . . as long as every member of your family is over the age of 18. **168 pages $11**

BB-118 "Crab Town" Carlton Mellick III — Radiation fetishists, balloon people, mutant crabs, sail-bike road warriors, and a love affair between a woman and an H-Bomb. This is one mean asshole of a city. Welcome to Crab Town. **100 pages $8**

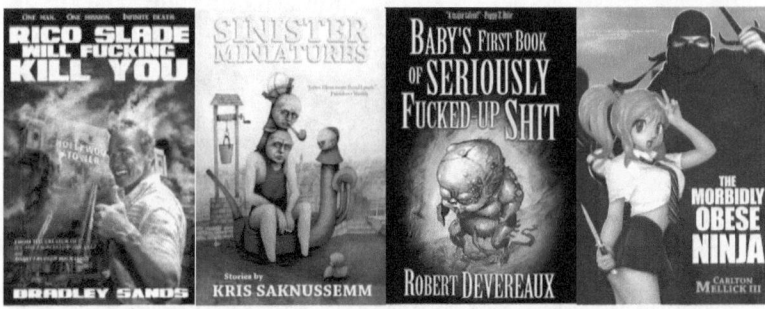

BB-119 "Rico Slade Will Fucking Kill You" Bradley Sands — Rico Slade is an action hero. Rico Slade can rip out a throat with his bare hands. Rico Slade's favorite food is the honey-roasted peanut. Rico Slade will fucking kill everyone. A novel. **122 pages $8**

BB-120 "Sinister Miniatures" Kris Saknussemm — The definitive collection of short fiction by Kris Saknussemm, confirming that he is one of the best, most daring writers of the weird to emerge in the twenty-first century. **180 pages $11**

BB-121 "Baby's First Book of Seriously Fucked up Shit" Robert Devereaux — Ten stories of the strange, the gross, and the just plain fucked up from one of the most original voices in horror. **176 pages $11**

BB-122 "The Morbidly Obese Ninja" Carlton Mellick III — These days, if you want to run a successful company . . . you're going to need a lot of ninjas. **92 pages $8**

BB-123 **"Abortion Arcade" Cameron Pierce** — An intoxicating blend of body horror and midnight movie madness, reminiscent of early David Lynch and the splatterpunks at their most sublime. **172 pages $11**

BB-124 **"Black Hole Blues" Patrick Wensink** — A hilarious double helix of country music and physics. **196 pages $11**

BB-125 **"Barbarian Beast Bitches of the Badlands" Carlton Mellick III** — Three prequels and sequels to *Warrior Wolf Women of the Wasteland.* **284 pages $13**

BB-126 **"The Traveling Dildo Salesman" Kevin L. Donihe** — A nightmare comedy about destiny, faith, and sex toys. Also featuring Donihe's most lurid and infamous short stories: *Milky Agitation, Two-Way Santa, The Helen Mower, Living Room Zombies,* and *Revenge of the Living Masturbation Rag.* **108 pages $8**

BB-127 **"Metamorphosis Blues" Bruce Taylor** — Enter a land of love beasts, intergalactic cowboys, and rock 'n roll. A land where Sears Catalogs are doorways to insanity and men keep mysterious black boxes. Welcome to the monstrous mind of Mr. Magic Realism. **136 pages $11**

BB-128 **"The Driver's Guide to Hitting Pedestrians" Andersen Prunty** — A pocket guide to the twenty-three most painful things in life, written by the most well-adjusted man in the universe. **108 pages $8**

BB-129 **"Island of the Super People" Kevin Shamel** — Four students and their anthropology professor journey to a remote island to study its indigenous population. But this is no ordinary native culture. They're super heroes and villains with flesh costumes and outlandish abilities like self-detonation, musical eyelashes, and microwave hands. **194 pages $11**

BB-130 **"Fantastic Orgy" Carlton Mellick III** — Shark Sex, mutant cats, and strange sexually transmitted diseases. Featuring the stories: *Candy-coated, Ear Cat, Fantastic Orgy, City Hobgoblins,* and *Porno in August.* **136 pages $9**

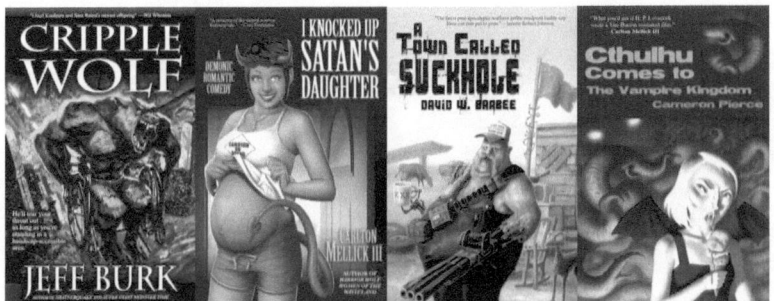

BB-131 **"Cripple Wolf" Jeff Burk** — Part man. Part wolf. 100% crippled. Also including *Punk Rock Nursing Home, Adrift with Space Badgers, Cook for Your Life, Just Another Day in the Park, Frosty and the Full Monty*, and *House of Cats*. **152 pages $10**

BB-132 **"I Knocked Up Satan's Daughter" Carlton Mellick III** — An adorable, violent, fantastical love story. A romantic comedy for the bizarro fiction reader. **152 pages $10**

BB-133 **"A Town Called Suckhole" David W. Barbee** — Far into the future, in the nuclear bowels of post-apocalyptic Dixie, there is a town. A town of derelict mobile homes, ancient junk, and mutant wildlife. A town of slack jawed rednecks who bask in the splendors of moonshine and mud boggin'. A town dedicated to the bloody and demented legacy of the Old South. A town called Suckhole. **144 pages $10**

BB-134 **"Cthulhu Comes to the Vampire Kingdom" Cameron Pierce** — What you'd get if H. P. Lovecraft wrote a Tim Burton animated film. **148 pages $11**

BB-135 **"I am Genghis Cum" Violet LeVoit** — From the savage Arctic tundra to post-partum mutations to your missing daughter's unmarked grave, join visionary madwoman Violet LeVoit in this non-stop eight-story onslaught of full-tilt Bizarro punk lit thrills. **124 pages $9**

BB-136 **"Haunt" Laura Lee Bahr** — A tripping-balls Los Angeles noir, where a mysterious dame drags you through a time-warping Bizarro hall of mirrors. **316 pages $13**

BB-137 **"Amazing Stories of the Flying Spaghetti Monster" edited by Cameron Pierce** — Like an all-spaghetti evening of Adult Swim, the Flying Spaghetti Monster will show you the many realms of His Noodly Appendage. Learn of those who worship him and the lives he touches in distant, mysterious ways. **228 pages $12**

BB-138 **"Wave of Mutilation" Douglas Lain** — A dream-pop exploration of modern architecture and the American identity, *Wave of Mutilation* is a Zen finger trap for the 21st century. **100 pages $8**

www.ingramcontent.com/pod-product-compliance
Lightning Source LLC
Chambersburg PA
CBHW020731250626
47155CB00006B/2245